DANGEROUS PLACES

Elaine Raco Chase

BANTAM BOOKS
TORONTO • NEW YORK • LONDON • SYDNEY • AUCKLAND

DANGEROUS PLACES

A Bantam Book / November 1987

ISBN 0-553-26544-X

Published simultaneously in the United States and Canada

Bantam Books are published by Bantam Books, Inc. Its trademark, consisting of the words "Bantam Books" and the portrayal of a rooster, is Registered in U.S. Patent and Trademark Office and in other countries. Marca Registrada. Bantam Books, Inc., 666 Fifth Avenue, New York, New York 10103.

PRINTED IN THE UNITED STATES OF AMERICA

KR 0 9 8 7 6 5 4 3 2 1

DANGEROUS PEOPLE

"I don't like people who violate me—"

Roman held up his hands. "If you call that kiss a violation, just wait until—"

"—or violate my surroundings." Nikki's thumb jerked inside. "You tossed my apartment. Discover anything interesting, Cantrell?"

"How'd you know?" Roman made an exaggerated inspection of the doorframe. "No popped cellophane tape. No broken matchstick. And if there's a fallen strand of your red hair, I'll be damned if I can find it."

"I have a sixth sense. You'd do well to remember that."

Roman grabbed her arm, hauling her in to face him. "And you'd do well to remember that *I* don't like to be violated either. Now, now, that wide-eyed innocent look does not become you, Nikki Holden. I found my lost driver's license under your desk blotter."

"What can I say?"

He smiled. "Thanks for updating the license photo with the ink mustache."

"You're very welcome."

The telephone sounded and Nikki grabbed it, hesitating with the receiver halfway to her ear. "Say, Cantrell, you didn't bug my phone by any chance?"

"Aw, shucks, I knew I forgot something."

Nikki gave Roman a smirk before answering the phone. "Hello."

"I hear you have company," came the resonant voice. "The man in question. Correct?"

"Yes."

To my parents, Ernest and Helen Raco, of Schenectady, New York, who never blinked an eye when their daughter went from Nancy Drew to Perry Mason and Mickey Spillane

DANGEROUS PLACES

Chapter One

"Dammit, will you listen to me?" Marcy Nathan jabbed her elbow into Nikki Holden's side and continued the painful bashing until Nikki put down her betting sheet. "Look to the right," Marcy said urgently. "See the big guy at the end of our row, three sections over. Black hair. Mustache. Burgundy shirt and navy slacks."

"So? What's the problem?"

"*Him!* He's the problem! He's been watching me, staring at me, following me for the last four days." Marcy spoke so quickly, so heatedly that her words plowed into one another, threatening to turn into a mere babble. "He's even been at the afternoon practice sessions."

"Marcy, you are paranoid." Nikki dipped her fingers into the tub of buttered popcorn that was balanced on the wooden arm between their two seats. "There's six thousand people coming into this fronton for the jai alai games tonight. Probably most of them were here watching the practice. It's been like that for the last month.

"A crush of people. Mostly bored people escaping from dull convention meetings or too little action at the dog races or just passing time between the last Follies show and the next one."

Nikki tossed some popcorn into her mouth and

chewed reflectively. "A veritable sea of faces and bodies. And you notice *one* guy? He's probably just some awestruck Midwesterner attending the pipefitters convention."

"Does he look like some frigging plumber to you?" Marcy's high, young voice screeched. She fumbled in her purse for another cigarette. "He . . . he doesn't watch the jai alai games. He watches me. Look at him!"

Nikki didn't look. She didn't have to. Marcy may have spotted him just this Wednesday, but she'd pegged him two days earlier. Tonight he was going to be her unwitting pawn. "Maybe he wants a date, Marcy, and he's a little shy," came her disinterested response as she pretended to refocus attention on her trifecta selections for tonight's million-dollar jai alai jackpot.

"No."

"Why not?"

"I'm committed to Ignace," Marcy stated emphatically.

"Your new admirer doesn't know that."

Marcy shifted uncomfortably. "I *know* it's not about a date."

"Really?"

"Yeah. He . . . he would have hit on me by now. I know where it's at; I'm a woman of the world."

Marcy Nathan. Woman of the world. Nikki gave an inward snicker before waving away a gust of cigarette smoke. Marcy Nathan imagined herself lots of things. She was, however, as phony as the ID she'd shown to get into Pleasure Island's jai alai fronton.

Oh, the plastic-coated Florida driver's license complete with photo did proclaim that she was Marcy Nathan, free, white, twenty-one, and short. What it neglected to reveal were the girl's invincible blond roots, adolescent chain smoking, the three studs that dotted each earlobe, and a teen wardrobe in colors that resembled a pack of Tropical Fruit Life Savers.

Nikki stared hard at Marcy's pouty mouth, and immature features that time had yet to define. Here was a little girl wearing bravado like a coat. Nikki had managed to open it wide, though, to reveal Marcy's vulnerability. Nikki hadn't been particularly cunning, just persistent. For the last four weeks she had courted Marcy Nathan, given the girl everything she hungered for.

It hadn't been fun. Painstaking. Trying. Annoying. But never fun. Nikki finally allowed herself to smile . . . slightly. But she wasn't in this for fun. *Just pure profit.*

Marcy had tried very hard to appear to be simply one more groupie who adored the jai alai players noisily and constantly from ten feet away. But her groupie image was as phony as her name. The girl was such a fake, Nikki thought, such a transparently obvious fake.

Once Nikki had confirmed Marcy Nathan's real identity, she knew she had gotten herself all the way to the tightly bolted, well-guarded door she'd sought. Effectively manipulating Marcy Nathan was her key to opening that door, behind which sat the prize Nikki Holden was determined to possess.

She took another look at the girl. Fear registered in Marcy's wide brown eyes. Nikki decided to move quickly to make that fear work to her advantage.

She selected a particularly large piece of popped corn and studied it carefully as she said, "If your mustachioed admirer isn't interested in a date, just what does he want with you?"

"He wants . . . he just wants me, that's all." Marcy turned to stare at Nikki. "It's a private matter. A secret."

"Then *you* handle it. Privately." She uncrossed

her legs and started to rise. "You're a woman of the world. You can—" But the multi-ringed fingers that locked around her wrist halted both her words and movements.

"I...I can't, damn you." Marcy's voice splintered. "I...I don't know how to handle someone...someone like *him*."

She watched Marcy light a third cigarette off the half-smoked butt whose filter tip had been pulverized. The girl was feeling pressured. All Nikki had to do was apply a little more heat.

But how much? There was no margin for error. She had to be perfect; she had to be careful. After that, there could be only success.

Her gaze shifted to the red and white striped popcorn container. Marcy was a lot like the kernels. Her tough shell was vulnerable to the elements. Too much heat could make her parch, shrivel. She'd be a dud. Unusable.

But with just the right amount of heat, the right amount of pressure, and a dab of oil, the girl would explode into something quite beautiful.

Nikki allowed herself a quick, casual glance at the man who turned out to be the perfect catalyst. Tonight he was careless. Obvious. Or maybe just unlucky. His physical features, posture, and self-assured manner were too damn overwhelming.

Who was he? Why was he here? Those were two questions that Nikki Holden needed the answers to. Needed? Hell, more than that—she was desperate for those answers.

This afternoon and evening she'd garnered the distinct impression he was more interested in *her* than in Marcy, and she decided now to turn his curiosity against him. That would give her an edge.

She sat back. Quiet. Thinking. Silently, she role-played a few scenes, trying to gauge Marcy's response and reactions. She'd made up her mind and was about to speak, when the momentum was stolen from her.

The jai alai players filtered into the protected pelotari's box and onto the court for their pregame warmup. The crowd took up the chant for their favorite: "Ignace. Ignace."

Even Marcy joined in. Adoration replaced fear on her face. Color returned to her cheeks, her brown eyes glowed, and the ever-present cigarette tumbled from her petulant lips.

When the twenty-three-year-old Basque player finally stepped onto the racquetball-style jai alai court, thousands in the audience went crazy. Ignace's reaction was the opposite of tradition. He acknowledged the response and began to show off.

The kid was quick. He had lots of arm, lots of leg. He was one of the best. Nikki watched him scale the concrete wall with a five-foot leap. He plucked the ball from the air with the slinglike wicker cesta strapped to his arm. The pelota, harder than a golf ball and three quarters the size of a baseball, came off the wall at speeds of at least a hundred miles an hour, ricocheting dangerously around the playing area.

The spectators roared. The chant was taken up again. Only louder. "Ignace. Ignace." Nikki smiled as the bad boy of the world's fastest and most dangerous professional sport stayed on the court two minutes longer than scheduled. He was giving the hungry bettors a tantalizing hors d'oeuvre of action to lose or win their money on.

Jai alai. Big business. Very big. Very beautiful. Very dangerous. The pelota can kill. Nikki wondered how the players could even see a ball that had been clocked at 175 miles per hour let alone catch it and hurl it back.

Jai alai players were anonymous, mere numbers to the crowds that cheered them on. Television commercials encouraged people to turn out for games but there was no coverage. Newspapers and radio stations reported little more than scores. Jai alai players didn't win college scholarships. They didn't do breakfast cereal commercials or underwear ads. They didn't pose for shirtless pin-up posters or appear in "do you know me" American Express card spots. Their fans didn't beg for autographed balls.

All that was scheduled to change. At least for one pelotari—Ignace. The angry young man whom crowds used to boo was now their darling. Ignace, soon to be a major sports star, was a potential gold mine for the operators of Pleasure Island.

Jai alai may have started in the Pyrenees Mountains of Spain, but one part of the game was pure Roman Empire. It is the only sport in the world where men bet on men. And Nikki Holden was about to wager four weeks' work on Marcy Nathan's love and fear of Pleasure Island's favorite pelotari.

The lighted odds boards changed quickly, all in Nikki Holden's favor. She reached into the popcorn box. "I've an idea, Marcy. Why don't you let Ignace handle your mustachioed mystery man? I bet he could—"

"No! No, that's not a good idea." The girl shook her head furiously. "I...I don't want Ignace involved. Couldn't you—"

"Help?" Nikki placed one kernel after another into her mouth while she pretended to think about the girl's plea. "Sure. I'll help. I've got a few secrets myself."

Marcy stared at her. "Yeah...yeah, I bet you do." Then her purple-tinted lips curved. "But I know your secret, Miss Investigative Reporter. You want an interview with Ignace."

She tapped out another cigarette. "And you can't get to him. I've been watching the way you operate. You're good." Marcy stroked her lighter to life. "But in the last four weeks you haven't been able to crack the security."

Her eyes narrowed at Nikki through the blue-based flame. "Has anyone talked to you? No. Not the managers, not the players, not even the cashiers. Miss Investigative Reporter has drawn a blank.

"But I can get you that private interview. That's what you've wanted from me all along." Marcy inhaled deeply. "You've been nice to me just to get an introduction to Ignace. I'm not stupid." Her lips twisted. "You want the interview, then help me handle this guy. He makes me nervous." Marcy's mouth drooped. "He's dangerous. He's unknown."

"I'd like to know a little something about him myself," Nikki mused. She didn't like unknowns any better than her companion. Unfolding the printed betting sheet, she held it up as if they were both looking at it. "It's nearly eight. The National Anthem will start in just a few minutes. As we sit back down, I'm going to spill that popcorn and I want you to put up a little fuss about me getting more.

"Once I leave, you wait five minutes and then look to see if our friend is still there. If he's followed me, you slip out the side exit, take a cab, and beat it back to my apartment."

"But what about Ignace? I'm his lucky charm, I've never missed a game."

"He won't know you're not sitting out here cheering," Nikki countered brusquely. "And if our mysterious friend is after you, he's done his homework. He knows you won't budge until Ignace plays and that would make him feel secure enough to see what I'm up to." Her blue eyes turned to ice. "Keep biting your lip like that and you won't need to eat. What the hell's the matter now?"

Marcy lowered her head, her dark hair curtaining her face. "I don't know, maybe I should just wait and see what happens. Maybe he's nobody, a nothing."

Nikki gave an easy shrug. "Okay by me. Wait and see. After all, he might be that horny plumber looking for a date I said he was to begin with. Oh . . . oh, he's moving closer, relocating himself right across the aisle."

The girl snapped to attention. "Shit." Marcy took a deep breath. "I hope I'm not making a big mistake trusting you."

"As far as I can see, I'm the only friend you've got. Is there anybody else you can call? Ignace?"

Marcy shook her head.

"Knowing what I do about your hot-blooded Spaniard, he's aptly named. A real fireball. He's probably all action and little communication."

She sighed. "He's not easy to understand."

"Isn't that exactly what he told you about his wife? The proverbial 'she doesn't understand me' line."

Marcy's lips thinned. "What do you know about it? We love each other and that bitch won't let him go."

Nikki gave her a speculative look. "Is that why you're so eager to keep Ignace away from this guy? Are you afraid Ignace's wife sent your silent admirer?"

The girl paled.

"Messy divorce cases make such interesting reading even in the sports section. That kind of publicity won't do Ignace much good with all his newfound wealth in contracts and endorsements." Nikki licked the salted butter off her fingers, her tone casual but cutting. "How about you, Marcy?

Could you use the publicity? Name and photo spread all over the newspapers. Think about that."

Nikki watched as the cigarette in Marcy's mouth was replaced by her index finger. She sucked thoughtfully for a long minute, defeat registering in her eyes.

"All right." Defeat was in her voice, too, now. "I'll do what you say and go to your place."

"When do I get to talk to Ignace?"

"I'll . . . I'll talk to him after tonight's game."

"Do more than just talk, Marcy," Nikki's words were heavy with warning. "Get me an interview with Ignace. Set it up. Fast."

Chapter Two

The bottled brunette was his target.

She hadn't been that hard to find. She'd changed her last name but not her first when she booked a flight from Las Vegas to Miami. Spotting her, then getting a positive ID on her had taken some time and had given him a headache.

He'd been looking at first for a blonde. One with Alice-in-Wonderland hair. Lady Clairol had obviously been called in; so had a scissors. Her hair was chopped shorter on one side than on the other. Although, knowing her background, he was sure both the color and the style had exotic names attached to them, along with a very large tab from a pretentious barber who called himself a "hair designer."

But it was her, all right. There was no mistaking that vapid, heart-shaped face, petulant mouth, sulky expression, and the child-woman body. She was calling herself Marcy Nathan and obviously had a faultless ID that boosted her age to the legal limit, if not beyond.

No matter. His job was done. He'd found her. Knew where she lived. Knew her daily routine. And confirmed her relationship with the jai alai player, Ignace. He could get Marcy Nathan at any time. Easily. And that's why he let his attention shift.

The redhead caught his interest. Caught and

held it for the last two days. He wasn't quite sure why. He had yet to discover her name.

Although she sat in the designated area, she certainly wasn't one of the hard-core jai alai groupies who flashed her qualifications night after night by the players' cage. Too old. He judged her to be close to thirty.

He was curious about her relationship with Marcy Nathan. They sat together both at afternoon practice and during the games. Shared food, like the popcorn tonight. Friendly. Chatting.

Maybe his interest was piqued by nothing more than the startling contrast between the two women.

Nearly a foot taller than Marcy, the redhead stood about five nine in those low-heeled, crepe-soled tan sandals, he figured. Unlike Marcy's cartoonish costumes that appeared cheap, loud, vulgar, and immature, the redhead's clothes were sleek and understated. She wore them; they didn't wear her.

Her body was both hard and soft. Strong. Supple. The sleeveless black sweater she wore tonight showed off shapely muscled arms, full breasts, and a slim waist. As they stood for the National Anthem, he noticed how her khaki slacks defined her long legs and rounded buttocks.

His dark gaze traveled the shapely route, finally coming to rest on her hair. Strands of copper and gold. Like a shiny new penny. Short and curly on the top and sides, waving to her shoulders in back.

He speculated on the fact that Lady Clairol might have done double duty. He'd personally volunteer to check.

It was her profile, though, that really intrigued him. Challenged him. He kept wondering why. Tonight curiosity gnawed harder, goading him into moving progressively closer to her. He settled himself one row behind her, just across the aisle. The redhead was less than five feet away. While she was making final decisions on her betting strategy, he was scrutinizing her features.

Her forehead was high, her squarish jaw well defined, chin strong. The fullness of her cheeks provided an attractive softness. An innocence.

He narrowed on a new target. Her nose. That's where her profile went sour. He kept staring. Puzzling. Suddenly, it came to him. He'd be damned! Her nose had been *broken*.

Now that really was intriguing... as intriguing as trying to find out the color of her eyes. So when she walked past him, still brushing popcorn off her clothes, he followed. Close. Confident that amid a full house of over six thousand, he'd be taken for just another handicapper eager to part with his money.

She moved nice and easy. From the hips. The steep incline down to the betting cages didn't deter her hip-swaying progress one bit. *Poetry in motion.* That corny line made him grin.

Abruptly, *she* changed his interest from personal to professional. Instead of continuing straight toward the concession stand and betting windows, she turned right to the public telephones.

Nikki smiled. He was hooked. She added a bit more sway to her walk. So easy. But that had always been true. P. T. Barnum had correctly called it: There's a sucker born every minute.

She was good at the con, good at the sting, good at having no conscience. He was just a little too sure of himself, a little too slick. She was going to enjoy watching him fall. "Hello, sucker!" came her muttered greeting as she lifted the telephone receiver.

Her fingers dug into the bottom of her black

leather envelope bag for the appropriate coin. A quarter clunked down the instrument's gullet. She casually shifted positions so he'd have to be blind to miss any of the numbers she was punching.

The redhead was being very careless, he thought. Or maybe, despite her age and her bearing, she was just as immature and brainless as Marcy Nathan. Then again, what did *she* have to be careful about?

His thoughts shifted back to Marcy Nathan. He hesitated, wondering if he shouldn't go back and mind *his* business. But Marcy never moved until after Ignace played and the redhead had started to talk. She had a very low, very seductive voice.

"Hi. Me again." Nikki made her laugh suggestive. "Sounds real good. No. No problems at this end. Everything's going perfectly. How's that again? I couldn't agree more. I'll call you later for further instructions. 'Bye."

Further instructions. His thumb and forefinger worried the thick, black mustache that fringed his upper lip. He decided to stick with her. Find out her name, her business, her involvement with Marcy Nathan. Unknowns had a nasty habit of fucking up a game plan.

Nikki straightened slowly before making a quick move toward the heavily congested lobby. He was right behind her. She was conscious of his every step. All she had to do was to manufacture the correct combination of events. Lord, the man was making things so easy.

Her first stop was to replace the tub of popcorn. Just to be perverse, she asked for extra butter. Then she strolled toward the betting windows, juggling the popcorn and her purse while taking the marked sheet from her pocket.

He stayed close. Feeling free because she was so

preoccupied. He found himself guessing at her picks, remembering how much time she'd spent going over her selections. Hell, he had the money. Why not put down a bet. He felt lucky tonight.

Picking the right line was important. Actually, it was finding the "right" people in the line rather than those with lots of dollars to bet that Nikki was looking for. The second line was populated by too high-class a group. Men in tuxedos and women in furs seldom made public spectacles of themselves. Her gaze drifted up and down, finally settling on the fifth line. There were ten people ahead of her, but the wagerer in the anchor position was going to be her winning pick. She angled a too-close-for-comfort position behind the short, bald-headed man.

He was perfect: Lots of gray hair foaming at the opened neck of his tropical sport shirt, glittering pinky rings on both hands, black socks and white shoes peeking out from seersucker trousers. It nearly killed her to breathe; his smelly oversized cigar had to have a deadly EPA rating.

The important fact, however, was that Tall, Dark, and Mustachioed queued in back of her. Seconds later, with all the unknown players in their proper positions, Nikki put her plan into operation.

She sandwiched herself closer to the man ahead of her. He kept puffing on his cigar, looking from her to his betting sheet and back to her again. Nikki smiled. He smiled back. His yellowed teeth were a dentist's nightmare; brown tobacco juice colored his saliva.

Nikki turned her gag into another seductive smile and added a wink. Baldy reacted as she had expected and moved toward her. She stepped back and deliberately stumbled over some nonexistent object on the floor. Popcorn flew like confetti. The cigar smoker decided to be a hero. "Hey, honey, be careful. Let me help."

"Oh . . . oh, dear . . ." Feigning off balance, she floundered for a second before taking yet another step back. "Oops! Sorry." Nikki felt rather than saw her quarry's hands lock on either side of her waist. His deep "Steady there" rumbled pleasantly in her ear.

Her purse headed toward the floor.

He caught it.

"Hey!" came her loud screech. "That man grabbed my purse!" Eyes wide, she clutched at the cigar smoker's beefy arm. "Help me. Please."

Cigar reacted just as she knew he would. He became her knight in smoky armor, taking a stalwart stance, ordering loudly: "Drop that! Hey! Guard! Where the hell's the security guard?"

"What the—" A startled expletive was muffled by the pressing crowd that chanted in unison for the guard and tried to help the tearful, hysterical redhead. In that instant, Nikki could tell that Tall, Dark, and Mustachioed knew he'd been had.

A uniformed security guard stepped into the crowd. "Okay, okay. Break it up. There's only five minutes to place your bets." He isolated Nikki and the muttering man she was fingering as a thief.

"All right, what's the problem here?" His right hand made a reflex move toward his hip holster; his eyes were a second slower in registering on a familiar face. "Oh, it's you, miss." He smiled warmly at Nikki. "What's the trouble?"

Sniffling, Nikki pointed at her purse, still clutched in the man's hand.

"You've got it all wrong." He looked at the guard's name plate and added with a smile, "Really, Officer Raines, this is just a simple misunderstanding."

Pete Raines sized up the man and decided to keep his hand on his gun. "Miss?"

"He...he probably has a collection of wallets ...other people's wallets on him." Her voice faltered on every word.

"Now, wait just a damn minute—"

The guard interrupted. "I think we'll just adjourn to my office and have a look-see." Pete confiscated the purse. "That way." He firmly ushered them toward a blue painted door. "You all right, miss? He didn't hurt you, did he?"

Nikki sniffed and gave him a weak smile. "No. I don't think so. It happened so fast." She put a hand on his arm as they walked the short distance. "He must be a professional," came her low whisper. "And what a bonanza in tonight's crowd." Nikki patted his arm. "Thank God you're around, Pete."

The guard gave her a smile. "I'm glad I could help *you*, miss. You've been so thoughtful and generous this past month. Bringing me coffee and doughnuts and sandwiches while listening to my stories."

Ignoring Mustache's rude snort, she beamed, "My pleasure, Pete, you're a very interesting man."

Reluctantly, he abandoned her arm to unlock the door with his passkey. "In here, mister. Keep moving." Pete pushed him past another guard, who was busy trying to keep an especially juicy hamburger from splattering the dozen video security monitors he was watching. "In there." Reaching around, he opened a glass door. "Now, let's have it."

"Have what?" His shrug was nonchalant, his manner relaxed as he leaned against the wooden desk. "The *lady* is mistaken. I did not try to steal her purse."

He had to give her credit. She was good, very good. When she looked at him, her eyes were chips of light blue ice. Cold and calculating. But to the guard they were awash with tears, making her look as vulnerable and irresistible as hell.

Nikki crowded against Pete Raines. "He followed me from my seat to the concession stand to the betting window."

"Well?" Pete charged.

His laugh was light, almost embarrassed. "Hey, I'm with the proctologists' convention and she has the cutest ass—"

"That's enough of that!" Raines roared. "Let's see some ID."

"Look, she's got her purse. Nothing's missing. So, what's the bitch?"

"Your ID." Pete squared his shoulders and made his voice more authoritative. "I'm the law in this fronton. I can arrest you just as legal as the police." He held out his hand and waited.

She moved closer to the guard's side when a driver's license was finally offered. "Roman Cantrell. Miami," Nikki read out loud. "I don't know, Pete. That picture doesn't look a thing like him."

"The mustache is new," Roman commented dryly. "What do you think?"

Her blue eyes narrowed their focus, her tone sarcastic. "I don't *think* this is your license. Maybe that's not even your wallet."

Pete grunted in agreement. "Let me see that." Before Roman had a chance to protest, the tan cowhide was grabbed by the guard, who began shuffling through its contents. "All the credit cards are issued to a Roman Cantrell, but that doesn't mean much. Nothing else with a photo on it." He breathed noisily for a minute, spreading the contents of the wallet on the other desk while he tried to figure out his next move. "Here, write your name. Let's see how the signatures match up."

"Brilliant idea, Pete," Nikki returned quickly, "you'd be able to spot a forgery."

Roman groaned, but at the guard's insistence turned to use the pen and pad on the desk. Pete spotted a second bulge in his back pocket. "And what do we have here? Another wallet? Looks like you were right, miss." Pete flipped it open, then hesitated. "Uh-oh." His indrawn breath was sharp. He stared oddly at Roman before turning toward Nikki. "He's a private cop."

"What?" She grabbed the license. *Private cop.* Her mind overflowed with implications. Now she knew she had to put Marcy Nathan somewhere safe. And fast. She certainly didn't need Florida's answer to James Bond screwing up her plans.

"I don't know, Pete." Nikki spoke carefully, trying to stall for time. "This license could by phony. You can order them from magazines. You'd better check him out with the Dade police. If he's for real, they'll know him."

She edged closer to the door, thinking and talking fast while making her actions casual. "You know, Pete, this could be a test. You were just promoted and this guy . . . why Cantrell could be a ringer . . . a phony . . . sent by management to check up on you."

As unobtrusively as possible she slid her purse and one other item off the desk. "You'd be wise to do a lot more investigating. I don't want to interfere; you handle this whole incident. For my money, Pete, you're doing one helluva job."

Before either man could utter a protest, Nikki Holden made her escape.

Pete Raines's fifty-six-year-old body was quickened by a mixture of fear and resentment. "So that's what this is all about, yeah? Mrs. Leonora Reichman and the Pleasure Island people don't think I'm qualified to handle this job? They send you in to see if this old man can spot—"

"Take it easy," Roman said, his voice as calm and soothing as he could make it. "I wasn't sent here to test you. And those credentials are real."

The guard hesitated. "I think I'd just better check with Captain Hutton." Pete lifted the telephone receiver.

"Fine with me. This time of night, Brian'll be home." He reached over and punched in the phone number.

Pete quickly disconnected the call. "All right. You convinced me." He removed his gray cap and wiped the sweat off his forehead, moist fingers running through thinning white hair. "Sorry about the misunderstanding. Not like Miss Holden to get confused and upset."

"Holden?"

"Yeah." Pete Raines opened the top desk drawer and hunted through a clutter of papers. "Here's her card."

NIKKI HOLDEN—CORTLUND PUBLISHING SYNDICATE.

"Reporter." Roman flicked the card, watching it somersault faceup on the tattered desk blotter. He grinned at Pete Raines. "I don't know. Anyone can have a card printed up. Did you check *her* out?"

Raines squared his shoulders. "Hey, I know my job, buddy, and this lady is A-okay." Brown eyes narrowed, making his face appear even more wrinkled. "Say, since you didn't know Miss Holden, then you were sent by Leonora Reichman to—"

Roman merely smiled. "Like I said before, I got sidetracked by her cute butt. See you around, Officer Raines."

Roman's first stop was to check on Marcy Nathan. The girl was gone. Cursing, he headed for the phone booth. Just maybe Nikki Holden had been careless letting him watch her dial that number.

Less than a minute later he grudgingly acknowledged that a quarter had just joined his lost dignity. His cautious hello was returned by a recorded message:

> "Lord, make me to know mine end, and the measure of my days, what it is; that I may know how frail I am." Today's verse is from the Book of Psalms, number thirty-nine, verse four."

Nikki Holden had made Roman Cantrell feel very frail indeed.

Chapter Three

Nikki edged her midnight blue Chevy Blazer into the eastbound lane on the Julia Tuttle Causeway, cautiously blending into the heavy evening traffic that was speeding toward Miami Beach. As the causeway curved into Arthur Godfrey Road, a riot of neon color provided a thin layer of tinsel over the graceful coconut palms silhouetted against the night sky.

She wasn't, however, susceptible to the view. Her thoughts and energies were concentrated on two people: Marcy Nathan and Roman Cantrell.

Marcy had to be her first concern. The young girl represented too much work, too much time. This was too major a coup to be handled carelessly now. Besides, Nikki silently consoled herself, she was totally confident about her plans in dealing with Marcy Nathan.

She was less than assured about Roman Cantrell.

The man was going to be a headache. Probably a migraine. Maybe an ulcer. Certainly high blood pressure. Nikki had realized that the minute he'd opened his mouth. Cantrell was quick on the uptake, sarcastic, and deeply relaxed. She grudgingly admired those traits. But admiration of one's adversary tended to be less than productive, less than profitable.

Nikki tried to focus Cantrell in her mind's eye and was angry at just how clearly his image developed.

His casual, carefree attitude, loose-jointed posture, and ready grin was a ruse in itself. There was a steely tension about him, an athletic build that belied his demeanor, and keen brown eyes that probed from lean, hawkish features.

Granted she had manipulated and outmaneuvered him tonight. But anyone would fall for a sucker punch. Once. Roman Cantrell couldn't be jockeyed twice. Nikki was quite aware that she was going to need a helping hand to stonewall this particular private investigator.

Private investigator. Nikki wondered who could have hired him. Was he really after Marcy? Or shadowing Ignace? Or had Roman Cantrell been sent to keep tabs on her, Nikki Holden? She had been annoyingly persistent in dealing with the Reichman Industries staff at the jai alai fronton. Then again, maybe it was something or someone altogether different.

That was an interesting thought! Difference was what she enjoyed. No, no, came Nikki's silent correction, *difference is what I feast on.* And Roman Cantrell just might prove to be another interesting appetizer to what was turning out to be a banquet of an assignment.

Nikki turned into Tidesfall's brightly lighted underground parking area. Her social security number was pressed into the numeric keypad control lock and a minute later the heavy gate rolled up to allow her access. After parking in the designated slot, she rode the garage elevator to the tenth floor, then used an extra key to gain entrance to condo number 1053.

The carved oak door slammed into an anxious Marcy Nathan. "Well? What happened? Who is he? What does he want?"

Nikki kicked the door shut as she looked beyond

the girl into a littered living room hazy blue with cigarette smoke. "I see you made yourself right at home." Ignoring Marcy's continuous barrage of questions, she left her in the foyer, briefly detouring to the kitchen for a wastebasket, then headed into the living room.

"I get hungry when I'm nervous," Marcy whined, trailing after her.

The first to be emptied was a free-form blue crystal bowl that overflowed with lipstick-ringed cigarette filters. The fresh fruit it previously contained had been tossed on a beige-cushioned rattan chair. Three soda cans clattered dully into the heavy plastic garbage can.

"I... I was expecting you sooner," the girl babbled, "or at least a... a phone call."

Nikki grimaced at the curdled bacon-horseradish sour cream dip that was dotted with broken potato chips. She chucked it, smashed the empty chip bag on top, then surveyed the carpet of crumbs that nearly obscured the design on the Oriental rug. "Believe me, had I known you were such a *tidy* person, I would have had you meet me at the landfill." The instant Nikki finished that verbal assault, she regretted it; even more so, when she saw the expression on Marcy's face.

"Screw you, lady!" Marcy shouted. "Hassled! That's all I ever get is hassled." She scooped up her purse, cigarettes, and lighter from the glass cocktail table. "First my old lady. Now you." She headed for the front door. "I don't need this shit." Her words and gestures punctured the smoky air. "I don't need you. I don't need anybody. I can handle it all."

"Good! Then you go right ahead and handle the private eye." Nikki watched Marcy Nathan stumble against the wall.

"A... a private eye?"

"Actually, I think they prefer the chic television nomenclature: private investigator." She smiled at the girl, then settled comfortably on the sofa. Directly above Nikki was a massive wall mural depicting a tiger elegantly pouncing into a thicket of bamboo palms.

Marcy moved like a sleepwalker. "Did you find out his name?"

"Cantrell. Roman Cantrell. Mean anything?"

"No." She lit a cigarette while edging into a chair. "Ahh . . . did he say who hired him?"

"Don't you know?"

"I . . . uh . . ." Marcy took a deep drag through the chambered filter. "Probably Ignace's wife. That's right! That's who it is! The little bitch." Twin streams of smoke bannered from her nostrils. She looked purposefully at Nikki. "I mean, who else could it be?"

"Who indeed?"

"It has to be her," Marcy said too emphatically. "She's like that. Vindictive. Nasty. She doesn't understand Ignace and—"

"Oh, yes, amazing the way 'she doesn't understand me' sanctions adultery."

Marcy's features were suffused with color. "Listen, you don't understand. We really love each other. Ignace wants a divorce but that bitch won't let him go."

The girl leaned forward, her tone low and confiding. "He's told me stories about his wife. Why, she's nothing but a cradle robber! The old bat says she's only fifteen years older than Ignace, but hell, she's close to being able to pick up her social security check. Cassandra. That's her name. Professor Cassandra Topping. She'd be a great interview for some shrink. Or—" Marcy's brown eyes narrowed thoughtfully. "You could go see her, Nikki, at that private girls' school in Boca Raton, where she teaches. You could talk to her, find out things."

"What kind of things, Marcy?"

"Oh, you know. About her marriage and does it bother her that she's so much older than her husband. How she feels about his new contracts and endorsements." Marcy settled back with a fresh cigarette. "You know, Nikki, that's the reason she's hired this private eye. She's afraid Ignace is going to dump her before she can get her hands on all his money. That's why she's going to try to get something on him."

"Blackmail?"

"Exactly."

Nikki's fingers drummed reflectively against the sofa cushion. "Could be. Ignace is certainly going to be reaping some major financial rewards."

"He figures a couple million."

The redhead whistled. "That much?"

Marcy fidgeted. "That...that was a secret, Nikki."

"Another secret?" She smiled. "I thought the two of us had gone beyond that stage." Nikki sighed when the girl lit up again, stood up, and switched on the ceiling fan. "When am I going to be able to talk to Ignace myself?"

"I—I said I'd talk to him tonight."

"I want more than talk, Marcy, I want the man himself."

The girl nodded.

"In view of your newest admirer, the private detective," Nikki translated, "I think you'd better spend the night someplace safer than your apartment."

"I could go to Ignace's."

"No, his place is probably under surveillance."

"How about here?"

Nikki thought about that for a minute, then decided against it. "No, Cantrell is just clever enough to get my name from the security guard at the fronton and pay me a visit." She walked over to a large oak desk that sat catercorner on the opposite side of the great room. "Let me make a call."

Fifteen minutes later Nikki hung up the phone and turned to Marcy. "I've arranged for you to stay across the street at the Crestfall condo. There's an underground walkway that connects the two buildings, so you won't have to go outside."

"What about Ignace? Nikki," Marcy pleaded, "I've got to see him. We usually spend the night together, and when he finds that I'm not at his place or mine, he's going to be frantic."

"You've got a point. Besides, you've got to talk to him for me." Nikki took a deep breath. "All right...how about this? You call his doubles partner, Carlos, and tell him where you are. Have him talk to Ignace in person and—"

"Why can't I just call Ignace?" Marcy interrupted.

"Because you can't be sure Cantrell hasn't tapped his phone. Call Carlos. Tell Ignace to take a couple of cabs and the polar route to the condo. That should shake anybody who's following him. Then you two lovebirds can spend a peaceful night together."

Marcy's eyes were gilded with admiration. "Say, you're pretty sharp. How do you know all this?"

"Just part of my overall health insurance plan."

It was midnight before she returned to the Tidesfall condominium. Marcy had been comfortably pacified in new surroundings with a six-pack of cola, a frozen pizza, and an R-rated HBO movie. Nikki supervised the call to Ignace's doubles partner and in an hour the jai alai player would add to Marcy's diversions.

Settled at her desk, Nikki pressed in the unlisted phone number of her own expert diversion-maker. On the third ring a gravelly voice issued a curt "Yeah?"

"Didn't wake you up, did I?"

"Wake me, no. Interrupt me, yes."

"My profound apologies to Rebecca."

"Don't be crude. What you interrupted was me reading the galleys of your NASA article for the next issue of *Science Realm*. Becky is in the kitchen unwrapping a late night snack from Taco Bell. Your favorite—nachos."

"That's low, Mathew." Nikki groaned. "You know it's an hour later here and everything is closed."

A deep chuckle assaulted her ear. "That's one of the perks of having an office in Chicago." Mathew Cortlund cleared his throat, his tone serious. "What's the problem?"

"Does there have to be a problem?"

"When *you* call me, yes."

Nikki sighed. "You're right. I do need your help."

"A major event but one I always appreciate. What can I help you with?"

"Roman Cantrell."

"Do we know him?"

"No. But I need to."

"Why?"

"He blossomed forth tonight and I need to know how to trim his thorns. Cantrell's a private investigator."

"I see."

She could hear background noises, a drawer slammed, shuffling. Nikki knew Mathew Cortlund was trading his magazine galleys for paper and pencil.

"Shoot."

"I'll read you Cantrell's Florida driver's license."

Mathew's indrawn breath was sharp. "You didn't."

"I did." As her index finger polished the colored plastic picture, Nikki's voice drowned out his mumbled curses. "Cantrell's got a chauffeur's license, issued June nineteenth of last year. That's also his birthday, the year was 'forty-nine. He's six foot, black hair, brown eyes. I'd put him about one hundred eighty pounds." Nikki rattled off his driver's license number and Fort Lauderdale address.

"I can't believe you lifted his wallet," Mathew muttered for the tenth time. "Dammit, Nikki, I thought—"

"That I reformed? Don't be silly, Mathew. Besides, it wasn't the whole wallet, just the license," she said consolingly. "And why the lecture? It's never bothered you before when I bend a few rules."

"Break a few laws."

"I prefer to create the odds, not play them. It gets you those exclusive stories that sell millions of copies of all those magazines you publish," came her laconic reminder.

"I thought, no, hoped you were mellowing."

"Nope." She laughed. "Not slowing down, not getting clumsy. Now, now, Mathew, stop all that sputtering. How dare you malign my talents! They've just landed you what may just be the story of a decade." Nikki sobered. "Any rumblings? Or are we still the only ones who know?"

"You're it, courtesy of that NASA launch engineer's fondness for champagne."

"I doubt a bit of the bubbly will work on Roman Cantrell. Of course, there's always a well-aimed cork. . . ."

Mathew heard her amused voice trail off. "Nikki" —his tone was sharp—"please try to be—"

"I try to be five steps ahead. That's why I need any information you can get by noon tomorrow.

Cantrell's going to come visiting and I'm going to greet him blind. I don't like that. I want an edge. I need to know his weak spot."

"Think he has one?"

"Everybody does."

"Just remember that."

"Well, almost everybody. What a lousy break! Damn, Cantrell, he's forcing me to move up my timetable."

Mathew cleared his throat. "Speaking of force. An old acquaintance of yours has invited himself into the picture. Remember Borgianno?"

"Rudy? What's a nice old mobster from Cleveland doing in Miami?"

"He's not there for a tan. Borgianno's reigning over the family's gambling and prostitution activities. It was a quiet takeover."

"The man is nothing if not polite. Low-keyed, not volatile, not a braggart. He treats people with respect."

"Sending a wreath and a mass card to the funeral is so Emily Post," came Mathew's sarcastic rejoinder. "He catches everybody off guard. It's his dapper Commander Whitehead facade."

"Rudy never fooled me. My article proved that. He does, however, have excellent taste. Sent me a two-pound box of Godiva chocolates and a bottle of Moët et Chandon."

"I'll let you expense-account a small greeting for Borgianno. Maybe he will tell you why he's so interested in jai alai."

"Is he?"

"Looks like it. There's rumblings again about fixes in a few games."

She was thoughtful for a long moment. "Maybe that's the reason everyone is walking on eggs around here. Trying to get an interview with even a janitor is impossible. So far the only employee I've locked into is the security guard. Nice old codger, seemed desperate for a friend. A very reliable gossip."

"How goes getting the interview with Ignace?"

"The Basque fireball is going to be a multi-million-dollar baby, and I'm assured of getting the full story tomorrow." Nikki scratched her cheek. She wondered if Rudy Borgianno was interested in Ignace. Maybe the mobster hired Roman Cantrell. "Any luck getting an interview with Leonora Reichman?"

"No. I finally got past her executive assistant only to be transferred to Paul Taylor, their corporate lawyer. He knows less than nothing, puts me on hold, I listen to elevator music, and then get cut off," Mathew said with disgust. "Leonora Reichman makes Fidel Castro seem like an extrovert when it comes to one-on-one interviews."

"Well, Queen Leonora won't be able to complain that we didn't give her the opportunity to do this the legitimate way," Nikki responded cheerfully. "Don't you worry your bald head about it. I've discovered the perfect backdoor to Leonora."

"I thought going through her million-dollar jai alai player and lover was your way in?"

"Ignace's turning out to be just plain cake, Mathew, I've found the frosting. I've found the guarantee. And when Leonora waltzes into Miami on Wednesday to play hostess at the Pleasure Island charity pro-am tennis tournament, she'll find me making an offer that is impossible to refuse."

"I don't think I like the sound of that, Nik."

"Have no doubts, Mathew. The interview is a sure thing." Suddenly, Nikki was swamped by a wave of unfamiliar giddiness. "God, Matt, I'm higher than a kite over this. Now I know how Woodward and Bernstein felt when they discovered Watergate wasn't a simple robbery."

"Well, this isn't so simple a story either, Nik, and it seems to be getting more and more complicated. When you do get to Leonora, ask the lady about the three bomb threats to her Las Vegas Pleasure Palace."

"Three? Hmmm...the first one made the papers and I assumed she was just on the Vegas strip extortionist's list. I know from talking with the security guard here that there have been no bomb threats."

"I've got confirmation that the Vegas operation has been a target three times. Her security people are excellent and well paid to hush this up. You can imagine how much money her casino would lose with publicity like that."

"Oh, I don't know, Leonora thrives on creating titillating publicity, she just never sticks around for the fallout," Nikki reminded Mathew. "Hell, she's gone through four husbands—"

"Six."

"Oh, yeah, I keep forgetting about the punk rocker and then there was that messy suicide of her last hubby, those nude photos." Nikki's laugh was hollow. "Somehow, Mathew, I doubt a few bomb threats would undo the lady."

"Ah, but don't forget about her upcoming venture. She's switched her allegiance from the Hollywood crowd to the Washington bureaucracy."

"Too true, too true." Nikki smiled happily. "You know, Mathew, what started out as just another million-dollar jock story has mushroomed into enough articles to keep at least five of your magazines jumping off the newsstands. And having the edge about what Leonora Reichman is *really* planning just may net me a Pulitzer!

"Hell, Matt, barring a nuclear war, this truly will be the story of the century. I can't believe the...the...hell, the godlike effrontery, the sheer impudence of that woman in circumventing state and local governments and going over everyone's head"—Nikki snickered—"way over everyone's head with a federally legalized scheme that boggles the mind."

"Take care with Queen Leonora; you've spent enough time on her background to know she's a cross between a shark and a barracuda, so watch out. I know you, Nik, you're on the jazz. You love all this intrigue and subterfuge and, well, frankly, your penchant for pushing the legalities and—what? Oh, all right. Becky said for me to stop carping and tell you that she won't ask if you're eating properly or if you liked the new clothes she sent to you and she hopes you didn't fire the housekeeper that she hired for the condo."

It was a little game Nikki allowed Rebecca Cortlund to play. The questions were always the same, always motherly. Nikki's answers were polite. "Yes. Yes. No. And thank her for not asking. Hey! Don't crunch those nachos in my ear! Mathew, you don't have time to eat. Get going on that Cantrell information."

It wasn't until she'd hung up the phone that Nikki remembered to add the mustache to Roman Cantrell's description. She picked up a felt-tip pen and carefully went to work on his license photo.

"There you go, Mr. Private Eye, now the face and the photo match." Her thumbnail scraped along her bottom teeth as she stared at Roman Cantrell's picture. "I don't know who or what you're after, but I'm not going to let you destroy my plans."

His dark eyes and lean features haunted her long after she'd finished her artistic endeavor.

Chapter Four

Roman Cantrell's Oyster day and date Rolex read Sunday, 7:01 A.M.

A minute behind schedule.

The condo's security system hadn't been the problem, he silently acknowledged. It had been the damn dead bolt on Nikki Holden's front door.

"Rusty. I'm getting rusty," Roman mumbled, glowering as he again glanced at his watch. "Just my luck to run into deep-cut cylinders." He'd spent fifteen seconds too long on his knees in the dusky hallway. The lock had taken a steel tension wrench and three needles to make it snap.

He silently eased himself inside and found the drape-shrouded apartment cloaked in sleep. The alcove on his right led to the kitchen. Roman ignored it. Instead, he long-legged it to the partially closed door at the far end of the massive living room.

Hand splayed against the polished oak, Roman paused and smiled. His mood was buoyant. Hell, he was positively triumphant. Nikki Holden may have outmaneuvered him last night at Pleasure Island's jai alai fronton. But not this morning. This morning he was the clever early bird that was going to make a red-haired worm wriggle.

His fingers snapped on an impulsive idea. He should have stopped for bagels and coffee. Nothing like enjoying breakfast in bed...no, a roll in bed with Nikki Holden. Roman's smile turned into a broad white-toothed grin. He inhaled deeply, chest expansive.

No frail man he. Not today. He slammed open the bedroom door. But the witty greeting he'd rehearsed deteriorated into a strangled "Oh, hell!"

The room was dark and empty. The covers on the queen-size bed thrown back. Her imprint crushed onto boldly striped sheets. Roman stepped into the master bath. His hand reached for the towel rack and confiscated an oversized white football jersey with Holden on the back. The colors belonged to the Chicago Bears.

The silky material still held body heat and the bathroom sink glistened with water. "At least I know what she sleeps in," came his chagrined rejoinder. He tossed the shirt back on the bed and grew thoughtful. "Where in hell could she have gone this early?"

Her Blazer had been parked in its underground stall. That meant wherever Nikki Holden had gone, she'd walked. Roman shook his head and crossed to the richly draped wall. "Probably went down while I was coming up." He parted the heavy material and was rewarded with a stunning view that stretched clearly for miles.

The rich blue Atlantic Ocean misted into the blushing horizon. The early morning sun cast a fiery glow on an anchored fishing trawler. Beach palms swayed in the breeze, casting moving shadows on the sand.

A white-suited figure sprinted across the condo's rear tennis courts and headed toward the beach access. Immediately, Roman knew who it was. He watched Nikki Holden headed north, copper braid swinging in cadence with her easy jog through the ruffled tide.

His annoyed expression was reflected twice in the dresser's double mirrors; the irritation he felt was with himself. Hadn't he spent the better part of the night on the phone collecting information on Nikki Holden. "Hell, I should read my own damn reports!"

But Roman had read the reports and puzzled over them, then abruptly dismissed them as inaccurate. Now the speculation and questions returned. As did Nikki Holden's allure, and the intrigue around her.

He flung himself onto the bed and stretched his rangy body into the identation she had left. "Small comfort," he said sourly, then smothered a yawn. God, he was tired. Angry too. And disgusted. Not to mention that his ego was decidedly bruised and battered.

Yawning again, Roman tried to release the tension that coiled within. His body and brain refused to cooperate. His thoughts and emotions totally impounded by one woman, his muscles vexed with a need for movement. He sat up, rubbed a weary hand over his face, flexed his shoulders, then shifted his attention to searching the premises.

The closet revealed a modest wardrobe, both in quantity and price. Coordinated sportswear dominated the handful of new dresses, their tags hanging like decorative ornaments. The clothes were colorful. More so than Roman would have imagined. He'd always thought redheads wore blue.

Odd items caught his gaze. A snowmobile suit and fur mukluks were pushed against the far wall along with other winter-weight clothing; hiking boots and a heavy-duty backpack had toppled sideways onto high heels and sneakers. Apparently Nikki Holden traveled well prepared for an assignment in any climate.

Roman advanced on the white wooden dresser. The top was clear. No jewelry box. No crystal perfume flagons. He yanked open two drawers at a time.

Jockey-for-Her briefs in size six and 38C underwire bras all in beige occupied one; slips, belts, and scarves the other. Tagged sweaters were in a third; a variety of oversized sport jerseys in a fourth. He took one out. The Red Sox baseball shirt was authentic. The last two drawers were empty. So was a six-drawer chest and both nightstands.

The bathroom proved just as barren. Roman pulled a long copper strand from the hairbrush on the counter and found the root held the same vivid color as the end. In the medicine cabinet sat a bottle of generic aspirin, an all-purpose first-aid kit, Arrid Roll-On, and Crest toothpaste. Under the sink were assorted towels emblazoned with the Tidesfall condo name.

One cabinet drawer was empty. The other contained a pathetic collection of cosmetics. Even his mother, a Nebraska farmer's wife, had owned more than this. He inspected the hand-sized plastic pouches and found they were nothing more than samples. One from Estée Lauder; the other from Revlon. A tiny ampule marked Shalimar rolled between his fingers.

Once again Roman viewed his frowning face in a mirror. He double-checked the undersink cabinet and added a box of Kleenex and a package of bathroom tissue to his list of discoveries.

Hands on hips, he tried to think what was puzzling him the most. What was missing? Then he had it. The total absence of any purely feminine products. No tampons or sanitary napkins; no douches; no contraceptives. "Not even a lousy hair curler," Roman muttered.

The telephone's caustic jangle shattered the silence. Then he heard Nikki Holden's lyrical voice murmuring from the living room and froze. Had he been so preoccupied with his search that he'd missed hearing her return?

The thick brown carpet quieted his running return to the bedroom door. He peeked around the corner. His arrival coincided with the beep of an answering machine. A gruffly issued "Call me" was recorded by the tape and by Roman.

He checked the recorder's automatic counter and found it was the first call of the morning. "Maybe I'll get lucky and someone more talkative will ring." Roman settled comfortably in the oversized chair and began inspecting the cluttered desk.

A new electronic portable typewriter sat on a rubber mat. He squinted at an unfamiliar Japanese name and a keyboard that resembled an airplane cockpit. The machine looked fast, efficient, effortless. Roman smiled slightly, remembering the American-made manual typewriter he'd seen on the shelf in her closet. Nikki Holden would have a backup.

Roman scanned through a jumble of papers. All seemed to be reference notes and background research on jai alai, covering its 300-year history to modern times. Assorted colored squares of paper were filled with what appeared to be hieroglyphics and probably was Nikki Holden's own form of shorthand that would be impossible for anyone else to decipher.

Her Rolodex was the size of a dinner plate and crammed full. He twirled the wheel, making random stops. The white cards held the private numbers and addresses of a vastly diverse group: Politicians, both here and abroad, East and West Coast celebrities, sports figures, broadcasters, and more indecipherable squiggles—names he could only guess at.

He checked the desk drawers. None were locked. Nothing of value inside. A portable file box was in the largest drawer. Alphabetized by the month. January's manila pocket featured a story on consumer fraud against senior citizens; February's, a profile on a Japanese businessman. March's was titled The New Patriot—Mercenaries for Hire; April's held a NASA space research and commercial rocket update. May was marked *jai alai* and was empty.

He filtered through another, smaller stack of typed notes. Nothing. Then on a hunch lifted the brown desk blotter.

Roman's own face stared back at him. His driver's license. "Hell, I didn't even miss the damn thing!" He returned it to his wallet. "Cute, Miss Holden. Cute and clever. Looks more and more like the information I have on you is correct."

His fingers drummed uselessly against the desktop. He wasn't sure what he had expected to find, but he'd hoped more than this . . . this nothing. *Nothing*. That was the perfect word to describe what he'd discovered.

Last night's frail man sermon echoed in his ears. Drumming fingers turned into a fist that landed a resounding blow to the desktop. He was tired. Out of sorts. Hungry.

Roman whirled the chair around, stuck his face between the drapes, and peered down at the beach. No redheaded runner in sight. "Well, hell, Nikki Holden, you are a lousy hostess. The least you can do is offer your guest a little nourishment." He pushed off from the chair and headed for the kitchen.

"Now, what would a jogger have in her fridge?" His hand paused on the wooden handle. "With my luck she'll be a health-food nut too. I bet I find nineteen cubic feet filled with crunchy breakfast yogurt, aloe vera and carrot juice, wheat germ, bran, tofu and"—Roman made a face—"bean sprouts.

"Aw, what the hell...take a chance...you can always make toast." Yanking open the door, Roman prepared himself to damn an attack of vitamin bottles. "Well, this is a pleasant surprise." He took a step closer, bending farther into the cold, frostfree interior.

"We've got Super Bowl supplies. Salami. Hard cheese. One...two...four sticks of pepperoni. Italian bread. Lots of fruit. Left over Colonel Sanders." He counted ten six-packs of soda: five RCs, three Sprites, two Mello Yellos.

There were three jars of pickles in the door holder, along with a small jug of milk and orange juice. Mayo. Butter. Half a dozen eggs. Three white cartons from a Chinese restaurant. No beer. No wine. No mixers.

The freezer revealed a storehouse of Old El Paso frozen Mexican dinners, along with a selection of Hungry Man entrées. "Cast iron stomach." But that didn't surprise him. Nothing would surprise him, ever, about Nikki Holden.

He made a pepperoni and cheese sandwich, thickly blanketing the wide slices of bread with French's mustard, then popped the top off a can of RC. As an afterthought Roman riffled through the kitchen drawers and cabinets but came up empty except for some canned Chinese food, a three-pound jar of Cracker Jack popping corn, and a hot-air popper.

Munching thoughtfully, Roman wandered back into the living room and looked around. The condo was an attractive unit. Bedroom and living room with a view of the Atlantic. Color scheme in browns, golds, and beige. Rattan and glass furnishings were above average in both design and quality. So were accessories like lamps and paintings.

His dark eyes fixed on the three interlocking panels that hung artfully above the sofa. The Oriental tiger scene engrossed and absorbed him. The tawny ready-to-pounce feline reminded him of another wily, cunning creature. Nikki Holden.

Feeling both anxious and energized, Roman checked his watch. "Hell, she couldn't still be jogging, she'd be halfway to Daytona by now." He tossed the empty soda can into the trash as he passed by the kitchen on his way out the front door.

The invigorating salt air further rejuvenated him. So did the sight of a well-curved female body. She was wearing a very modest white maillot. Lying faceup on a blue surf rider. Eyes closed against the sun. Full breasts rising and falling in the steady rhythm of sleep.

He could still surprise her. Still deliver his witty rejoinder. Shit, this game of one-upmanship was juvenile, he thought. Hell, it was absolutely asinine.

Yet, Roman Cantrell approached Nikki Holden in stealthy, silent caution.

Chapter Five

"Frailty, thy name is woman!"

"Not last night it wasn't, Shakespeare."

Roman had expected Nikki Holden to jump. Be surprised. Flustered. Expected? Hell, he should have known better. Her eyes remained closed. Her expression serene.

"What brings the Noble Roman tiptoeing across the sand so early this morning?"

The only part on her moving were her lips.

His frown deepened. Despite the fact he towered over her supine form, Roman realized *he* wasn't the one in control. A different tactic was needed.

"I thought it was time to meet Nikki Holden, up close and personal." He strived to keep his mood light, tone bantering. "Seems you are the Barbara Walters of the printed page."

"Don't I wish I got her salary."

"You're known for taking a rumor and turning it into front page material."

"Not rumors, Cantrell. Tips. We in the trade call them tips."

Only Roman knew he was grinning. "Say, I'm not annoying you, am I?"

"Not in the least, but don't stop trying." The air-filled float she was lying on magnified the sounds of shifting sand. Cantrell had positioned himself close behind her head. Nikki sensed his staring.

She refused to open her own eyes and she knew why. She didn't want to see his face. She didn't need to. It was easy enough to visualize his mouth, resolute and tough, beneath the trimmed, thick black mustache. A mouth that could easily be transformed by a roguish, disarmingly attractive grin.

Easy. Yes. Much too easy.

His deep, measured voice did things to her. Warm things. Much hotter than the sun. She was stronger, though. Her breathing rate didn't change. Calmly, Nikki waited for him to make the next move.

Roman's thumb and forefinger massaged his mustache in a reflective gesture. Abruptly, yet in one fluid movement, he settled Indian-style on the sand. He rescued her braid from confinement beneath his legs and draped it over his calf. The vivid copper plait glinted contemptuously against his tan twill trousers.

"I was up most of the night collecting information on you."

"AT&T will erect a monument in honor of your phone bill."

He reached into his shirt pocket. "You certainly fill a notebook."

"My unauthorized biography? How flattering."

"Not all of it." Her smile paid him to continue. "You either have friends or enemies. Nothing in between."

"And they all told you the truth. At least from their respective points of view. Why don't you start this eulogy with the enemies." Nikki hesitated only a second before continuing. "I bet you talked with a colleague of mine, Carlisle."

Her eyes remained closed. Roman watched as her mouth quirked in a lopsided smile. "Colleague? I'd say he sounded more like a competitor. But the man was a proverbial fountain of information."

"Good old Ted. His cup does runneth over. Babble actually. He gossips more than any *man* I know. Discriminates against people without college degrees. Despises women reporters. Thinks a woman's place is beneath him. In a bed. Eyes glazed with ecstasy, body quivering with unbridled passion."

"Please, nausea does not become you."

She laughed. The sound was warm. Rich. Genuine. "Was I turning green?"

"No. From where I sit, you're tan. Very nicely tan. No freckles."

"Not a one. Why don't you call Carlisle back and tell him that? Then he can be your enemy too."

"So good old Ted volunteered to lead a freckle search, did he?"

"On numerous occasions."

"And?"

"If he had, wouldn't he be on the friends' list?" Nikki brushed away a pesky fly. "Let's see. Teddy would have told you that I was one of those castrating female reporters. A bitch. A backstabber. Used anyone and anything to get what I needed. Hmmmm . . . perhaps you *should* transfer him to the friends' list."

"You find that complimentary?"

"For a journalist all that counts is results, Cantrell. The field is tough and competitive. It's the *first* story that's remembered. The groundbreaker. I break a lot of ground."

Roman wiped his forearm across his forehead. Sweat clung to the curly dark hairs. "A rock star in L.A. would like to break every bone in your body."

"That skinny little no-talent runt? Ever hear him sing, Cantrell? He screams obscenities instead of lyrics. And not even in key. Onstage, he throws blood and excrement at the audience."

"To each his own. His fans know what to expect. Hell, they pay enough for a seat."

"True. So then, what's his complaint? He wanted publicity. I gave it to him."

"He says you're guilty of character assassination."

"I just printed his own words. He committed verbal suicide."

"You thrust your avenging pen into Roy Groveland."

"And just in time too. What a neat racket he had going! Gold scam. He'd already bilked investors in Oregon out of two million dollars." Nikki manufactured a sigh. "Isn't there anyone on my friends' list, Cantrell?" She smiled as she heard the exaggerated rustle of pages.

"Pete Rose."

"Good old Number 44 . . . it would have been nice to have Ty Cobb there, too, but—"

"Muhammad Ali gifted you with a poem."

"Better than a punch."

"And according to Miss Emma Brighton in Grand Rapids, you are a saint."

"Nice woman. Did you know some bastard was going to charge her forty grand to get rid of canker of the brick? He told her it was contagious to humans and fatal. Say, I hope you didn't wake Miss Emma up last night."

"No. A librarian friend of mine was kind enough to show me some of your articles." Roman waited to see if that would crack an eyelid. It didn't.

"My, my, you were such a busy boy."

"You're an interesting subject."

"Am I?"

"Lots of incongruity."

"Split personality, perhaps?"

"You're too tough to split."

"No, Cantrell. That's a mistake. I'm not tough. Not tough at all."

"No?"

"Nope. Tough can be dented. Eventually broken. I'm flexible. Resilient. Resourceful. I just keep adapting."

"And conforming? Like a chameleon."

"I wouldn't go that far. Chameleons practically disappear into their surroundings."

"You're right. No one could ever accuse you of disappearing."

Nikki detected a subtle change in his tone. "Aw . . . Cantrell . . . you sound tired. Out of sorts. Poor guy. Up all night. Big phone bills. And now, well, here you are sizzling on the beach." Her tongue clicked against the roof of her mouth. "What's the problem? Getting too much sun?"

"Too much cleavage."

She allowed herself another laugh. "Let me alleviate your discomfort." Eyes firmly closed, Nikki rolled over, cradling her head on crossed arms. "That better?"

"Much. I—"

"What's the matter? Sand fleas biting?"

"No."

The deadliness branded into his one word gave Nikki her answer. He would be asking more questions. She waited. He'd need time. Everyone always did.

Roman stared. Brown eyes widened. Then narrowed. Disbelieving. Blinking. Still doubting, he angled for a closer inspection. At first he'd thought the sun had indeed muddled his weary brain. But slowly and more clearly he began to assimilate just what his eyes focused on.

The white maillot was slashed to the base of her spine; thin straps criss-crossed bronze skin oiled by perspiration. The flesh above her shoulder blades was smooth, silky; the flesh below was not.

Scars. He'd seen them before in Vietnam. He even owned a few. But not this many. None this vicious.

To the left of Nikki Holden's backbone were a half-dozen shiny, puckered white circles. On the right, a wide crescent-shaped red keloid. Scattered between and disappearing under the opaque swimsuit material were raised netted welts and a multitude of faded white lines.

He wanted to touch her skin, magically to make the scars disappear. But he didn't. It took him a while to get his emotions under control so that he sounded normal.

"Somebody didn't like you a helluva lot, lady. Who was it? Ex-husband? Lover?" Roman answered his own questions. "No. I don't think you'd let a man do that to you. Who then?"

"You're the detective. Isn't this in your notes?" When he failed to respond, her mouth twisted sardonically. "How insufficient of you, Cantrell."

"Maybe not. I think this explains what I thought was an error."

"Error?"

"To coin a trite phrase, you've got a police record as long as my arm."

That statement caused a reaction.

She turned her head, opened her eyes, and looked straight at him. The effect was staggering. Roman watched her prismatic irises change into flame-sparked chips of steel. "The Saratoga Springs police department has two thick files with your name on them."

Nikki's expression was impassive. "That's real old stuff, Cantrell. You must know somebody."

"I *always* know somebody, someplace."

Et tu, came Nikki's silent rejoinder.

Roman thumbed through tiny notebook pages. "You certainly kept the village police busy. Started running the streets when you were six. Truancy. Suspended from school at age ten. Formed your own street gang when you were eleven. Habitual runaway. Parents and school officials were at a loss to know how to handle you."

"Ahh... the sins of youth."

"You ran numbers. Busted for shoplifting at nine, big stuff too—"

"Actually I started much earlier, they were just slow to nail me."

"—stealing purses from underneath restroom stalls—"

"You'd be surprised how careless the horse racing crowd is."

"—worked up to grand theft auto by sixteen—"

"I still maintain the owner greatly inflated the book value on his 'sixty-nine Chevy."

"And then, my favorite, aggravated assault."

"Someone aggravated me and they found themselves assaulted." Nikki smiled at him.

Roman grinned back. "Is that a threat?"

"Is there any trait about me you don't admire?" Her smile broadened, his leavening personality was heady and too damn attractive. That could be dangerous.

"You picked up more and more bad habits with each term in the detention center."

"Those are the only kind of habits to have."

"The only things not listed on your rap sheet are prostitution and drugs."

"My body's a temple. Only I say what goes in and out."

"Quite the juve, weren't you, Red?"

Nikki's tone became hard. "I have a name, use it!"

"And you still have a sarcastic mouth, a break-the-rules attitude, a—"

". . . a troublemaker since the day she was born, a short fuse, hair and eyes gifted from the devil . . ." Her mimic was two octaves higher. "That's what a Saratoga old-timer told you, wasn't it? Some people's perceptions never change."

Roman said nothing. His gaze strayed from her face to her back. "I know what detention centers were like eighteen years ago. Hell holes with often sadistic matrons. Punishment that was pain for the recipient, pleasure for the giver."

"Where oh where was Father Flanagan when I needed him?"

He made a disgusted sound. "Damn it to hell, Nikki, I'm serious."

"I know you are, Herr Doktor Freud. You figure I was so bad that the system had no choice but to beat law and order into me?" Her laugh was hollow; she shook her head. "Oh, well, I will agree with you about one thing, Cantrell, my cleavage is hard to take, especially lying down." Nikki levied herself up off the float into a sitting position. "And so's the sun. I'd hate to freckle this late in life."

Her movements were strong, lithe, straightforward. Just like her attitude and speech. Even though her bathing suit molded a curvy form, she was neither coy nor blatantly sexual. In fact, Nikki Holden didn't seem to be aware of her sensuality. Which made Roman more conscious of it.

There was an underlying vitality and excitement in this woman. And mystery. She was provocative. He was getting more and more intrigued. Hell, he realized he was damn captivated. Obsessed. He kept wanting to know more.

"What's between you and Mathew Cortlund?"

Nikki replaced the surf rider in its outdoor bin. Turning to face him, she was alert, wary, and on the defensive. Cantrell had found out far too much about her in eight hours while she had little knowledge about him. "I *work* for the Cortlund Publishing Syndicate."

Roman stood, brushed the beach off his clothes, and sauntered to her side. "I didn't ask about your work. I asked," he said persistently, "about you and Mathew Cortlund."

She pried his notebook from his hand and replaced it in his shirt pocket. Her fingernail traced one of the thin red lines that brightened the dark blue material, stopping over his heart. "You already know that answer too. The only way you could have gotten such old information on me was to have talked with . . . mmmm . . . Hutton or Fields or another retired cop in the Village. Hutton's my bet." Nikki smiled when his eyelids flickered. "That man hated my guts. He told you that I was paroled in Cortlund's custody when I was seventeen."

"Seventeen and a half," Roman amended. "You just missed doing hard time."

"Did I?" Her fingernail stabbed into him. "Cantrell, you're a bit of a defective detective. You really should check the accuracy of your information. One view doesn't make for the truth." Nikki stepped well out of reach of his suddenly circling arms.

He watched her amble across the tennis courts with long, easy strides. He had lots of questions and answers. But were they the right answers? Head lowered, chin pressed into his chest, he tried to identify his next move, made his decision, and caught up with Nikki Holden just as she reached the rear elevator. "All right. Why don't you correct me? Tell me what really happened. Let me hear your side, let me hear the rest of the story."

"God, now you're turning into Paul Harvey!" Nikki taunted, pushing the red button. The door opened immediately and she stepped inside. "Besides, aren't you getting off the track a bit, shamus?"

Roman followed her. "How's that?"

"I'm not the person you were hired to follow. Or am I?" Arms folded, she leaned against the carpet-upholstered wall and enjoyed the ride to the tenth floor.

"Was I hired to follow somebody?"

"Please, don't insult my intelligence, Cantrell. The only thing I want to know is who hired you."

"Don't insult mine, Nikki Holden. If I had a client, and I'm saying *if*, that information would be confidential."

The elevator doors opened. "How about if I run down a list of names and you just say 'no comment' when I say the correct one?"

He grinned. "No comment."

Nikki contemplated her options for a moment. "Maybe we could arrange an exchange."

"Yeah?" His shoulder touched hers as they walked down the corridor. "What kind of exchange?"

She paused by her door and turned to face him. His brown eyes were riveted to hers. His gaze never wavered, not even when her fingers dipped between her breasts to retrieve the key. "Information." She inserted the key in the lock, twisted the bolt free but didn't push open the door. "No sense in both of us spending valuable time gathering wool for the same sweater when we can—"

"Whoa! I think you're trying to knit a third arm on that sweater. I just went to a jai alai game and saw a pretty face I wanted to get to know."

Nikki's laugh was sarcastic. "You fracture me,

Cantrell. It took you four days to make a move on me?" She saw his eyebrow lift slightly. "I spotted you on Monday."

His lips spread into an easy smile. "Actually, I noticed you last Sunday. But I'm a shy guy." Roman nodded. "Say, why don't we adjourn inside? Maybe you can give me some pointers on improving my pickup technique over breakfast and—"

"Ahhh, you want a little verbal intercourse with your General Foods International Coffee."

Roman laughed. "Sure, make mine Cafe Irish Creme," came his insouciant reply, remembering one item in her kitchen pantry. "Say, you can never tell, my shyness may turn you on." He stepped nearer. "And eventually we could do more than verbalize." His index finger skittered across her collarbone. "You fascinate me, lady. You're sharp and fast and clever. Pretty damn clever last night."

Nikki pointedly ignored his touch, kept her tone light and even. "Like shooting fish in a barrel."

"Anytime you'd like to stuff and mount me." Suddenly he grabbed her shoulders, pulling her hard against him.

She took a lot of holding. Her body was strong; her muscles taut. His arms secured a stronger position around her slender waist. His eyes became mesmerized by her generous mouth.

Her breath came quickly between parted lips. Lips that were much too near to his for serenity. His actions surprised her. She'd missed all the cues. How stupid! Or was it deliberate?

Nikki felt his lips nuzzle the curve of her jaw, his mustache a sensuous tickle across her skin. His stroking hands flowed along the curve of her waist, moving slowly toward her thinly covered breasts.

His touch was strong yet gentle. His movements languid and unhurried. She was totally relaxed. Her own feelings subjugated her usual cautious instincts. Quelled her fears. When she spoke, her voice was nothing more than a moan that whispered his first name.

He never mixed business with pleasure. But Nikki Holden had gone beyond his definition of pleasure to personal. He readily acknowledged that fact the instant they kissed.

Her mouth was soft and yielding beneath his. Just as her body was in his arms. His lips and caresses became increasingly insistent. He elbowed open the apartment door. "Let's go inside and—"

Roman felt her pliant body undergo as rapid a transformation as her expression.

Chapter Six

"I don't like people who violate me—"

He held up his hands and took a retreating step backward. "If you call that kiss a violation, just wait until—"

"—or violate my surroundings." Nikki's thumb jerked inside. "You tossed my apartment. Discover anything interesting, Cantrell?"

"How'd you know?" Roman made an exaggerated inspection of the doorframe. "No popped cellophane tape." He looked up at her from his crouched position on the threshold. "No broken matchstick. And if there's a fallen strand of your red hair, I'll be damned if I can find it."

"I have a sixth sense. You'd do well to remember that." She calmly stepped around him.

Roman grabbed her arm, hauling her back to face him. "And you'd do well to remember that *I* don't like to be violated either. Now, now, that wide-eyed innocent look does not become you, Nikki Holden. I found my driver's license under your desk blotter."

"What can I say? How about old habits die hard?"

His mouth flowed in an easy smile. "Thanks for updating the photo with the inked mustache."

"You're very welcome."

"I think we were discussing coffee?" He released her.

Her hand made an encompassing gesture at the kitchen, her tone sarcastic. "Help yourself. I'm sure you know where everything is."

"*Mi casa, su casa.*"

"That's not my motto." The telephone sounded, and Nikki sprinted to beat the answering machine.

"Probably the same man who called before."

Roman's cheerful pronouncement caused her to hesitate with the receiver halfway to her ear. "Say, Cantrell, you didn't bug my phone by any chance?"

His face peered at her from the pass-through. "Aw, shucks, I knew I forgot to do something."

Without hesitation, Nikki believed him but honored Roman with a smirk before connecting with the person on the phone. "Hello."

"I hear you have company," came Mathew Cortlund's resonant voice. "The man in question. Correct?"

"Yes. I understand you called before." She pulled open the drapes, flooding the room with sunshine, then settled on the corner of the desk.

"You know I never leave any message. I do, however, have lots to tell you."

"Go ahead."

"First, inquiries have been made about you back in Saratoga. Old files were pulled and information lifted—"

"Yes, I know."

"Lots of questions about your current status too."

"Right."

"Don't sound so impatient, Nik. I realize I'm late with this, but had you answered the phone earlier..."

She laughed. "Sorry." The tantalizing aroma of perking coffee wafted into the living room. "But I know all about me."

"And I have someone who can fill you in on Roman Cantrell and treat you to Sunday brunch at the same time. You'll have to drive to Fort Lauderdale, though."

"No problem. I planned on heading in that direction today anyway. I've another link in this story to interview. Tell me the particulars."

"The Crab Shanty on U.S. One at eleven-thirty. You'll be meeting a federal agent assigned to the organized crime task force, so you're getting reliable information."

"I'm impressed, Matt. I knew you had connections but—"

"Don't compliment me too quickly."

She puzzled briefly over his statement. "Is that why you haven't mentioned a name?" When Nikki heard Mathew stutter, she knew she wasn't going to like his next words. "Now, now, Cortlund, you know me, I'd interview Satan if it meant getting a lead."

"Satan. Well, this name will ring a hellish note. How about Lazarus."

Her breathing grew noisy. "Why not? This has been my day for resurrections." Nikki tried to keep her tone light. "Well, hell, Matt, it can't be the judge. He's too old. . . ."

Matt laughed. "No, not Jake. His son."

"Son! What decent woman would have gone to bed with that crusty, ill-tempered, blindered old fart?"

"Nik, believe it or not, the judge was quite the ladies' man. Jake the Rake. On our hunting trips to Calgary, he always bagged more than a moose."

"Probably had syphilis. No wonder his sentences were so damn ridiculous." She scratched her cheek. "Lord, what's his son like?"

"Alex is definitely not a chip off the old gavel. You two have lots in common."

"Really?"

"Yeah. Jake sent you to reform school and Alex to a military academy."

"Alex got an easier deal and better food," she returned cheerfully. "Does he resemble his father?"

"Complete opposites. At least he was when I saw him at his bar mitzvah. Alex was the husky football type—blond, affable personality. Still has that, at least on the phone. He's very interested in meeting you. Especially after the glowing physical description I gave. So as Becky's always reminding you, look and act like a lady. Hey! I heard that snicker."

"It's the only comment I'm at liberty to make right now," Nikki parried. She regarded Roman, steaming mugs of coffee in each hand, as he cautiously made his way toward her. "Anything else?"

"One thing." Mathew's tone altered. "Against my better judgment but knowing and anticipating your next request, I put the word out that you'd like an audience with Rudy Borgianno. So you can expect some visitors."

"Why, thank you, Matt, that was very thoughtful and right on target. Uh-oh, I better go. Cantrell's face is contorting with pain from holding the hot coffee cups."

"You're not playing spider-and-fly with that man?"

"That's right, although we can't seem to agree on who's who," she returned. "I'll talk to you later." Nikki peered into the proffered cup and shook her head. "Tut-tut, Cantrell, better recheck your illustrious notebook. That's not how I take my coffee."

Roman set his cup on the desk. "Okay, what's the complaint?"

"It needs three sugars and lots of milk. While you're being a good detective and making a note of that"—she patted his cheek—"I'll slip into something a little less damp and sandy." Nikki slid off the desk and ambled toward the bedroom. Roman's ensuing question halted her in mid-stride. Hand on the doorframe, she turned her head. "Did I hear you right?"

The dangerous glint in her eye almost made him retract his question. "Yeah, I asked how'd you break your nose?"

Nikki felt as though all the air had left her lungs. She took a deep breath and forced herself to relax rather than react. "Not *how*, Cantrell. *Who*."

"Who?" He swallowed hard, already hating himself. "All right. *Who* broke your nose?"

"Which time?"

"How many were there?"

"Three. Four. Maybe more. I lost count." She pushed open the door.

"You didn't tell me who."

"No. No, I didn't." Nikki slammed the door and locked it.

The hot shower and rough soap scrub didn't wash it away. Neither did brushing her teeth twice with mint-flavored toothpaste.

Hate. It had a feel and a taste all its own. It could choke and consume. Or energize and propel.

Nikki Holden had lived it both ways. Opted for the latter. But there was always and would always be an aftertaste. Some days were destined to be more bitter than others. Especially when someone or something forced the past to intrude into the present. She washed the toothpaste foam from her mouth then leaned into the mirror.

Her nose. Becky Cortlund was constantly at her to get it fixed—for the last twelve years. Mathew went so far as to assign her to interview a famous Beverly Hills plastic surgeon.

Subtle.

But Nikki liked her nose. And her back. Wore them proudly. Purple Hearts. So her response was always deliberate obtuseness.

But that foil wouldn't work with Roman Cantrell. He kept hammering away. Picking at her. Hell! Nikki wondered why she'd even bothered to lock the bedroom door. He'd pick that too.

She definitely had to do something about Roman Cantrell. Just who could have invited him into the picture? Whom was he after?

Nikki quickly recalled the subjects. Ignace. Cantrell could have been hired by his wife to get divorce material. That would clarify his interest in Marcy, the prospective corespondent. Then again, since she knew Rudy Borgianno was interested in Ignace, perhaps Cantrell was a syndicate watchdog.

Her tongue clicked against the roof of her mouth. There was also Leonora Reichman and the Pleasure Island establishment. Cantrell could be undercover security and that certainly would explain why he was sitting in her living room. Nikki gave a satisfied grin, then murmured, "We investigative reporters are thorns in people's sides. Especially people with secrets."

Hopefully, Alex Lazarus would give her an insight into Roman Cantrell. Something she could use to deflect his assault. Maybe even a more accurate lead on Cantrell's target. Then she'd be able to adjust her own plans so there would be no further screwups.

Nikki blotted her face with a towel. "Hmmm, maybe I'd better do something about this nose. Hate to have another man preoccupied with it," she mumbled, tossing her small cosmetic collection on the vanity.

Nikki had learned a lot interviewing that plastic surgeon, but it was a question/answer session with a Hollywood makeup artist that proved more useful. Granted the makeup man was creating "movie monsters," but he'd shown her some clever camouflage techniques that she adopted whenever the occasion forced her to become Becky Cortlund's version of the perfect lady.

Perfection. An easy achievement with the proper tools. Nikki selected her colors and applied them effectively. Shadows and lights created optical illusions. Eyes dominated. Cheeks were slimmed. Lips glistened. A nose was straightened. Shower-damp red hair was pulled and twisted in a high off-center knot anchored with invisible hairpins and spiked by cloisonné chopsticks.

She slid into underwear, stockings, and heels. Clipped the tags from a dress Becky had sent, zipped it on, grabbed her purse from under the bed, and prepared herself to face one final problem: Roman Cantrell.

Roman had decided to pursue a new tactic in dealing with Nikki Holden. Make her come to him. That's why he ignored the opening bedroom door, refused to glance up from an intense reading of the Sunday *Herald*, and pretended not to hear the sound of her polite cough.

Of course all that changed when a whiff of seductive perfume attacked and quickly destroyed his strategy. He swiveled around—"Well . . . well . . . well . . ."—and looked her up and down, his gaze lingering appreciatively on her finer feminine attributes as he rocked back and forth in the chair. "You certainly know how to dress for breakfast."

"So, you approve?" Her pirouette was flawless.

"Most definitely." He scrambled from behind

the desk. "Why don't we adjourn to the dining room. I'll get the coffeepot and—"

"Don't bother for me." Nikki moved smoothly past him toward the entry foyer.

"Say...wait a sec...are you...Hey! You're going out."

She laughed more at his hangdog expression than at his flustered accusation. "Very good, Cantrell."

"What about us? Coffee. Chat."

"Haven't you been reading about caffeine? Terrible stuff." Her fingers closed around the doorknob. "And be honest, Cantrell, would you have answered any of my questions with anything other than 'no comment'?"

He grinned. "No comment."

"Ring around the mulberry bush is not the way I start my days."

"Where's your sense of adventure?" Roman gave her his best leer. "You're a clever woman. I'll bet you have all sorts of interesting ploys that would wear me down and make me talk."

"Then you'd *moan* 'no comment.' Now, don't take it so hard. Go back to the kitchen, sprinkle a little salt on your peter, and calm down." Nikki wiggled her fingers.

"Hey, wait a minute." But she moved too fast and Roman found himself locked in. His fist punched the door as he shouted, "This is not good for my ego." He sighed, a rueful smile twisted his lips. "What the hell! I broke in. I can break out." Just to be perverse, he did return to the kitchen, drank the entire pot of coffee, and ate the last two pieces of pepperoni in Nikki Holden's refrigerator.

Chapter Seven

Alex Lazarus quickly decided Nikki Holden made impressive watching.

Leaning comfortably against the chair's high cane back, he regarded her as she made slow progress crossing the Crab Shanty's crowded dining room.

She was taller than he'd expected. Even after he'd mentally subtracted her hairstyle and high heels.

More curvaceous. The toast-colored dress took its shape from hers and showed off a terrific pair of legs.

Carried herself like she could handle anything.

And was unmistakably vital. It showed in her walk and, as she came closer, in her expression. Her face, Alex mused, was distinctive and definitely attractive. An intriguing blend of wholesome sexiness. He couldn't, however, avoid noticing the impertinence that registered in her unusual eyes.

But it was her handshake and voice that added to his overwhelming favorable reaction. Her grip was firm, almost masculine, palm dry. When she spoke, her tone was rich and eloquent. She made his name sound sensuously attractive.

Nikki would have to tell Mathew Cortlund that Alex Lazarus hadn't changed much since his bar mitzvah. The adolescent huskiness had evolved into a muscular build. His hair remained blond and was cut almost military short. His handsome face still retained its boyish quality. But you could see the strength etched around his mouth and his dark blue eyes.

While his height matched hers, his body harbored an enviable grace that made his movements fluid yet controlled. His easy, open manner and ready smile made her feel calm and relaxed. In fact, with only a handshake and some nonpartisan chitchat, Nikki realized she'd taken an instant liking to Alex Lazarus.

"I've read and enjoyed your articles," Alex complimented her after they'd ordered Bloody Marys and crabmeat-topped eggs Benedict. "Uncle Matt makes sure every magazine he publishes ends up in my mailbox."

"He's very big on gift subscriptions," came her easy rejoinder. "Matt tells me you're on the organized crime task force."

He nodded. "I'm up here doing a little repo work." At her inquisitive expression, he added, "A house and yacht. Their owner used them in commission of a felony. Drugs. That makes it possible for us to confiscate them under the federal Racketeer Influenced and Corrupt Organizations law."

"The RICO statutes," Nikki said. "A reporter friend of mine did a story on one of your auctions. You guys do a multi-million-dollar business."

"We score a few points."

"Your father would approve." She decided to charge ahead and gauge his reaction.

Alex snapped his napkin to life. "Ah, yes, my father. I understand his judgmental hand was busy guiding the course of your life too."

"Guiding?" Her eyes left his face to focus on the hanging baskets of ferns that intimately sequestered their booth. "Dictated. Decreed. Ruled." Nikki's attention shifted back to Alex. "The sound of his gavel still echoes through the hallowed halls of Saratoga's circuit courtroom."

"His gavel often echoed against the seat of my pants," he returned with a wry grin. Alex took the drinks from the waitress's tray, handed Nikki one, and clicked glasses. "From one rebellious teen to another. I'd say we triumphed despite the old lecher's direst predictions."

"That we did." Nikki appreciated the Bloody Mary. It was cold, spicy, and loaded with vodka. "How was the military academy?"

"Tougher than Army Ranger School." He took a long pull of his drink. "About on par with your stints in reform school."

"Oh, you mean you had deluxe accommodations too?"

He laughed. "I see your peppered manners are finally cracking through that professional patina Uncle Matt warned me about."

"Touché." She hesitated before adroitly steering Alex in a new direction. "Is that where you met Cantrell? In the army?"

"I suppose you could say the army introduced us." Alex began buttering a crusty roll. "We shared a bamboo prisoner-of-war cage in Laos. During the rainy season. Not exactly the Hilton."

He let that simmer while the waitress served their orders and fussed over them the required amount of time to guarantee a twenty percent tip. "What's going on, Nikki? Are you after background material? Trying to score a few points and dazzle Roman with your diligence and determination. Is all this leading up to an interview?"

"Interview?" Nikki put down her knife and fork, propped her elbows on the table, and stared into Alex's face. "Now, I guess I could tell you that interviewing Roman Cantrell is what this is all about and you'd believe me. You know why, Alex? Because I'm a great little liar. Even your father never doubted a thing I told him. It's these eyes."

She smiled as she watched his Adam's apple bob nervously. "But I won't lie to you, Alex. I'm going to tell you the truth. I don't want to score points with Cantrell. I don't want to interview the man. I want to stonewall him so hard that I dent him. And for that I need information."

He blinked, coughed, and swallowed hard. "I thought... I mean I just figured you needed an introduction."

"Cantrell and I were introduced last night." She sighed. "He blundered in and nearly sabotaged the setup for a story that makes Watergate look like kid's stuff.

"Look, Alex, I've spent more than a month working one particular angle. Now, thanks to Cantrell, my timetable is shot and my source is nervous and unpredictable. I'm having to apply too much pressure too soon." Nikki viciously speared into the sauce-covered eggs. "Dammit, that man's a nuisance."

"Nuisance. Yes, that word certainly describes Roman. He annoys his way into places, into people's lives. Keeps at it. Hacking away. Of course, that's why he's so successful."

"Successful! At what? Playing James Bond."

Alex laughed. "James Bond? That's a good one. I usually tease him about being Sam Spade." He chewed for a reflective moment. "Seriously, though, Roman's well-liked and, more important, highly respected by law enforcement officials on all levels and in every state."

"What's his forte?"

"Lately, anything and everything. But his specialty is locating missing persons. Roman has a ninety-three-percent success rate." Alex noted her expression. "I see your interest is piqued. Where shall I begin?"

"How about the middle," Nikki prompted. "That way you can go backward and forward at the same time."

He took a moment to organize his thoughts. "About eight years ago Roman got word that he was needed back in Nebraska on the family farm. The war that had been going on between his father and his younger brother, Tony, had literally blown the Cantrell family apart. His brother had run off, his father was in the hospital recovering from a heart attack, and his mother was understandably distraught and confused.

"So Roman went home. It was his first time back in the States in ten years. Quite a culture shock. When he walked in the front door, he had another. There, time had stood still. The farm work, the land, the morals, the attitudes of rural Nebraska, hadn't changed.

"He quickly understood the discord and turmoil that had developed between his father and Tony. His brother wanted to see the world, experience everything he'd read or watched on TV. His father couldn't see the need for any changes. What worked for generations still worked. The land was all that mattered. Roman stayed until his father recovered, then after arranging for farm help, went searching for Tony."

'That was a pretty cold trail," Nikki interjected.

Alex nodded. "The trail got even colder and more beaten when Roman discovered just how many millions of kids had used it. Nearly two million kids disappear each year, Nikki. Sure, a couple hundred thousand are stolen by noncustodial parents. But the rest, well, the rest are abducted by strangers. There's your high fatality figures. Others are runaways who seem to vanish.

"Until a few years ago, police departments seldom took note of 'runaway' notations on the wire, and I'm sure you know that stolen cars were given a higher priority than stolen children. The FBI didn't get involved until twenty-four hours had passed and kidnappers made a ransom demand."

Nikki pushed aside the remains of her lunch. "Did he find his brother?"

"Yeah. Tony was a virtual prisoner at a religious cult that operated on the Vermont-Canadian border. Roman got him out, along with a dozen others. The kids spent quite a bit of time with psychiatrists getting deprogrammed.

"Roman had run into a few scams during the months he spent tracking Tony. He helped close down two kiddie porn operations, a child prostitution ring, and a handful of drug dealers. He freely aided police and government officials whenever he found anything."

Alex took a healthy swallow of his drink before continuing. "Five years ago Roman opened an office here in Miami, recently added three branch offices staffed with carefully selected operatives in Atlanta, L.A., and Manhattan. He's damn good at what he does, Nikki. Roman Cantrell can be your best friend or your worst enemy." The straight ends of his mouth curved upward. "But that statement describes you too."

"That statement can describe anyone," came her dismissing comment. "Let's have you fill in a few gray areas, Alex. You said Cantrell dealt mostly with missing persons. Kids. Runaways. But he does handle other cases?" Nikki carefully controlled her breathing while waiting for his answer.

"Definitely. Especially in the last few years, when

the Missing Children Hotline started and the FBI began using their Quantico, Virginia, computer in the VICAP program. Roman's taking on anything that interests him."

"What would that be, Alex? Security? Divorce? Corporate spying?" She grimaced as he attested to them all.

That doesn't help me one bit, Nikki thought. *Cantrell could have been hired to find Marcy, or to check security at Pleasure Island, or by Reichman Industries, or by Ignace's wife, or, for that matter, to keep me from nosing around!*

"I see that information wasn't too helpful," Alex commented, then added, "Roman is like a clam where his clients are concerned."

She decided to try another angle. Her tone was casual. "How about any vices? Is he a gambler? A lover? A doper? A lush? What are Cantrell's weaknesses?"

His expression hardened. "Lighten up, Nikki, the badger game won't work on him. Roman's none of the above. He's a nice guy."

"Okay, okay." Holding up her hands in defeat, she eased the mood with a laugh. "Can't blame me for trying. Like I said before, Cantrell's interfering with a story that's destined to become a history-making event. He's a nuisance. A fly in the ointment."

"No bug spray will touch him."

Nikki picked up her fork and resumed eating, watching as Alex did the same. She became alert to his every nuance. Waiting until his jagged breathing had normalized, color returned to his whitened knuckles, and the muscles and veins in his face and neck relaxed.

When she finally spoke, she adjusted the timbre of her voice. Making sure it was husky yet melodically soothing. "You know, Roman Cantrell *would* make an interesting story. That ninety-three-percent recovery rate is terribly heroic." Nikki saw Alex smile. "I remember you saying that Cantrell hadn't been in the States for ten years. Did he go off and join the Peace Corps? He certainly wasn't fighting in Vietnam all that time."

"No. Not 'Nam."

She pounced on that. "But fighting?"

His nod was hesitant.

"So Cantrell was fighting. Not in Asia...but somewhere, right? He...he...well, I'll be damned..." Nikki stuttered into silence. Suddenly she grinned. "You know, Alex, it's really amazing I didn't meet him at the soldier of fortune convention last September. I did a piece on mercenaries. That's what he was. Right, Alex? A mercenary." Her expression turned quizzical. "How about you? Were you one too?"

"Yeah. Me too. For a while." He finished his drink before looking at her. "So now what do you see when you look at us? Men covered in blood, dead bodies dragging from our heels? A hired killer? Assassin? Slay-for-pay. No...no wait, I think the new expression is Rent-a-Merc."

Nikki arched a titian brow. "Don't look to me for absolution or vilification. I haven't figured out whether I'm for or against paying for red, white, and blue covert work." Her fingers wrapped comfortably over his balled fist. This time, the softness of her voice was not an affectation. "Tell me how you and Cantrell got involved."

"It...it was harder for me than for Roman. Maybe that's why I lasted only a year. We went to Nigeria. Basically we were so-called neutral mercenaries running medicine and food for the Red Cross and church groups into Biafra. And...well...aw, hell"—Alex grinned—"we did throw in a few loads of guns for the Biafran military from time to time."

"How did you two *lobos* get started?"

"Both our outfits had been doing odd jobs for the CIA in Laos. Running guns. Setting ambushes. Blowing bridges. We worked both sides of the enemy lines when you could tell where the lines were.

"Anyway, that little episode in the prisoner cage was a setup—at least for Roman it was. He was the point man. Three very long days later the rest of his Green Beret unit showed up at the temple that had been turned into a prisoner camp. They freed what was left of our platoon and managed to nail four high-ranking NVA military types who had shown up to participate in the fun and games of interrogation.

"Roman was part of a freewheeling, arrogant Beret unit. He was enjoying it. A big contrast to the regular army code of behavior he had at West Point. And, I'll confess, Nikki, I was envious. They were trained to do anything, anytime, anyplace, anyhow. They did that and more and they did it with style."

Reflectively, he massaged his jaw. "Because of their assignment timetable, Roman assimilated the five of us. To be honest, it was heady stuff. It was *Indiana Jones* with Steven Spielberg directing.

"War is explosive. Fast-moving. Totally unpredictable. It's a minute-by-minute lifestyle. That adrenaline rush gets into your blood. You get a natural high. One you want to keep."

Nikki nodded. "I certainly understand that feeling."

Alex's laugh was short, biting. "Yeah, I bet you do. Well, what can I say? It was hard to give it up. I ran into Roman on R&R in Hawaii while we were both waiting to head back home. Of course you remember the kind of greeting the Vietnam vets were getting. Nazis and Japs . . . hey, that was an okay kill, you came home a hero, you came home to tickertape parades.

"Us? We were baby burners. We were, hell, we were lots of things. So instead of coming home to that, Roman heard of a profitable soldier of fortune unit headed for Africa and we signed on. Like I said before, I lasted a year and then headed home.

"Roman stayed in Africa and ended up training a guerrilla unit. Then a Central American coffee company signed him on for some high-risk security operations. We kept in touch. He asked me to visit his family in Nebraska. I did. His mother called me when trouble started up there and—"

"You contacted Roman," Nikki finished, then eyed Alex curiously. "Do you think Cantrell would have stayed away permanently? Just kept on living the roaming life of a mercenary?"

"I can't really answer for Roman, Nikki. I do know he was exceptional at what he was trained for."

"That being?"

"Demolitions, weapons, communications, some medicine and intelligence. Especially the latter. He was a skilled hunter and tracker back on the farm. Won some prestigious shooting competitions. As for staying a paycheck soldier..." Alex shrugged. "The pay is damn good. Cash up front and in a good bank. In Central America you make sure you have lots of American or English personnel around you. There is no wanton killing. No excessive brutality. No major atrocities."

"You're just on the side of whoever pays."

"That's right," he said. Looking at her pointedly, he added: "The word *mercenary* takes on a different inflection depending on the side of the person saying it. Lafayette worked with George Washington, the Flying Tigers were in China, and the

Eagle Squadron flew with Britain's RAF. They were mercenaries too."

Nikki smiled. "Alex, I always keep an open mind. If there's one thing I know from vast personal experience, it is that circumstances can alter any position and nothing is ever a simple black or white. As for moralizing or judg—"

"Nikki? Nik..." Alex watched her transformation. It happened in an instant. Her posture went from casual to military straight, her every muscle was tense and ready for action. Her expression hardened, her eyes never left his face, but they changed color. Turning from twinkling blue to ice.

Her back was toward the dining room, giving Alex the advantage. Yet she was the one who first acknowledged the approaching intruder.

"So this is the person you got all dressed up for this morning," Roman's tone was effusive and ebullient. "I don't know...." He studied her carefully, then grinned at Alex. "Sorry, pal, I got the better deal. I saw her in her bathing suit." Swinging a chair around, he parked himself at their booth.

"Now, isn't this cozy?" Roman inclined his head toward Alex and stage-whispered, "Have you checked your wallet? Miss Holden is very light-fingered. I know this from personal experience. Oh! If looks could kill! Look at her, Alex, those eyes of hers are very expressive weapons. Last night they held a touch of larceny. Right this minute it's homicide."

Alex was indeed staring at her. "Listen, don't jump to any conclusions, Nikki. This was not a setup. I did not tell him that I was having brunch here with you."

"Too true," Roman agreed. "But, and I'm sure Nikki will attest, old habits die hard. This is your favorite hangout, Alex. Mine, too, for that matter."

"Yes... yes, Cantrell." Nikki relaxed and smiled

at him. "I can see how this place would be a favorite of yours. All these lush ferns and palms, the tropical decorations. As I see it, the only thing missing from this charming scene to make you feel truly at home is Muzak playing *God Bless Nicaragua*."

His laugh was quick and clean. "I love the way you bounce back. You're right, you are resilient and not a sore loser."

"I haven't lost anything yet." She watched Cantrell confiscate her drink.

"And don't intend to?"

"A very perceptive statement."

Roman bit off a piece of celery and chewed reflectively. "So, what's the word on my unauthorized biography? I'm sure you charmed all the facts out of Alex."

"At least they're accurate facts."

"The ones on you aren't?"

Nikki contemplated the sensual movement of his mustache as he again crunched into the celery. "Why don't you ask Alex? Or better yet, his father. The judge knew me well."

"Is that a fact?" Roman eyed his friend.

"I seem to be caught in the middle," Alex muttered. He reached for his glass, found it empty, and hastily signaled the waitress for another.

"An uncomfortable spot to be in," Nikki agreed, "but one easily rectified." She got to her feet. "No... no, don't stand up." Her hand settled heavily on Cantrell's shoulder. "Alex, it was a pleasure to meet you. I hope to see you again. I don't mean to eat, gossip, and run, but I have another appointment and I'm sure you two have lots to discuss."

"Say, what about me?" Roman chimed. "Don't I rate a personalized good-bye?"

Her expression was as sarcastic as her tone.

"Good-bye? I wish! Unfortunately, I always seem to be saying hello to you."

Alex was the first to break the silence as Nikki exited from view. "Like that, is it?"

"Like what?"

"Don't try and snow me, Roman, I see it in your eyes."

"That lady could be a hard habit to break, Alex. We do have a lot in common."

"How's that?" Alex inquired, sipping his fresh drink.

"Well," he drawled, "for starters we both wear Jockey briefs." Roman winked and stood up. "See you later, pal. I've got to play catch-up with our friend."

Chapter Eight

Boca Raton was thirty miles north of Fort Lauderdale. Nikki knew the Atlantic was on her right. Occasionally, in between towering beachfront condos and sprawling mansions, she did, indeed, catch a glimpse of the rolling blue surf.

The ocean wasn't the only thing she'd glimpsed. Nikki's gaze darted from the windshield to the Blazer's below-eyeline side mirror. The Jaguar was still there. A sleek, silver specter that hovered in the distance.

She had noticed him about fifteen miles up on A1A. Him? Who else could it be, Nikki had decided, but Roman Cantrell. "Damn nuisance," she muttered for the hundredth time.

But was Cantrell following her just to be annoying? Or because he didn't know where she was going?

Nikki suspected the latter. Because if he'd known her destination, he could have beaten her there by taking the Interstate. And when she arrived, she would have found him sitting on the sports car like a hood ornament, his lips curved in a superior grin.

Then again, perhaps, he thought, by following her, she'd think just that and be fooled. Hell, she saw *The Sting*. "In fact, I've pulled a few stings. So watch out!" came her ominous warning.

Roman Cantrell was a challenge. Nikki knew he

was attracted to her and knew she could lead him on. But how far? To what end?

His attraction puzzled her. Men usually turned tail and ran from her barbed personality. She made men nervous, confused, always on the defensive.

An effective ploy to keep from getting involved. That's what Becky Cortlund always said. Becky was right. Nikki had spent her adult life striving toward proper, goal-oriented professional achievements. All her emotions were directed at her career. Until last night.

"What a difference a day makes!" she murmured. Now it seemed all her emotions were focused on Roman Cantrell. That was a mistake, but a mistake that was easily rectified. It was time to concentrate on the next item at hand. Nikki did just that, quickly and efficiently.

Holding up her notebook, Nikki squinted at the scribbled directions she'd taken down. She summoned up Cassandra Topping's lyrical voice stating—"You can't miss the house, it's right on the beach side. Number eleven. I'll leave the gate open." *Can't miss the house!* "Famous last words," Nikki groused as she stepped on the brake and began slowing down the car.

Cassandra Topping, Ph.D. Professor and head of the Department of Theater Arts at an elite Boca girls' academy. The lady was also Ignace's wife.

But what type of wife was she?

Jealous? Enough perhaps to hire a private investigator to dig up divorce material that would get her a six-figure settlement and ruin her husband's sports career?

Or maybe the professor and the jai alai player had one of those open marriages. Each free to enjoy other lovers, then drifting together whenever the mood struck.

Nikki was intrigued by the information she had uncovered. Ignace, at twenty-seven, was ten years younger than his wife. She was from a socially prominent southern family; he was a street urchin, an orphan with a wicked playing arm. They had met two years before in Spain, when Cassandra was on sabbatical and Ignace had just graduated from the Basque country jai alai school.

There was no denying the "Fireball's" impatience both on the court and off. Instead of going the regular route of a year of competition in Spain, Ignace jumped into western hemisphere competition.

Of course, Nikki amended, that jump was made easier since he'd married an American citizen who resided in Miami. Miami and jai alai—always the winning combination. A very profitable combination for Ignace. But for his wife?

The professor had been very gracious when Nikki called her from the lobby of the Crab Shanty. She'd even been invited to lunch. An offer she regretfully had to decline.

Nikki considered that for a moment. It was almost as though Cassandra Topping had been expecting her call. Maybe she had. Perhaps informed by a private investigator?

Again, she searched the rearview mirror for the Jaguar and found Cantrell was a quarter mile back. She watched him shear that distance when she abruptly turned into number eleven's brass-markered beachside drive.

Shielded from the main road by a well-manicured jungle of palms and brush pines, the mansion spread weathered brick wings across the ocean palisade. Old money. Nikki heard the echoes; recognized the trappings.

Of course, when old money fell into new hands, sometimes it kept slithering straight through. Nikki considered this as she parked the Blazer by a granite sundial with a baseplate engraved TOPPING 1925 and waited for Roman Cantrell.

"A Jaguar. How very Hollywood of you, Cantrell."

"Four-wheel drive. How very country of you, Holden."

"It comes in handy when the going gets muddy." Nikki looped her arm into his, laughed at his surprised expression, and discovered an exhilaration in keeping him off balance. "Well, this does work out nicely."

"I didn't realize you could purr."

She squeezed his bicep. "Now you can introduce me to your client."

"Client?"

"Oh, you do that wide-eyed innocent look too."

Roman smiled at her. "Sorry, Nikki, you're on your own." He patted her arm. "I'm afraid you'll have to handle all the introductions. In fact, I can hardly wait to see what that creative mind of yours comes up with." His finger pressed the door chime; a uniformed maid ushered them into the foyer.

"Miss Holden."

"Professor." Nikki extended her hand to the woman who quickly entered. She felt as if she were looming. Cassandra Topping was barely five feet tall. She seemed even more petite in a voluminous white gauze pants suit. Her face was fragile porcelain canvas framed by a white rolled turban. "Thank you for receiving me on such short notice."

"Not at all." Cassandra turned her green gaze on Roman. "This is?"

He smiled and turned his head toward Nikki.

Watching his smile turn into a devilish grin, she remained coolly undaunted. "I'm sorry, I often forget about my shadow. This is just one of our staff photographers." When Nikki saw Cassandra's blond brows arch, she hastily added: "Oh, don't worry, he won't be shooting today. Just looking around and making notes on the lighting."

"Good." Her laugh was airy, musical. "We're quite informal and rather lazy on Sundays. I do wish you'd been able to join us for lunch."

"Us?"

"Yes, we share a mutual acquaintance who's still here." Cassandra led them into the living salon.

It took Nikki only a second to recognize the lanky, dark-haired figure clad in a graffiti-covered romper. "Sybyll Fields!"

"Hello, Nikki, it's been a long time."

"Since Mount Saint Helen's erupted." Nikki gripped the offered hand with undisguised enthusiasm. "And congratulations on winning the Pulitzer for that photo series on famine in Ethiopia. The portraits, the faces were . . . well . . ."

"I know." Sybyll patted her hand. "I'd always photographed objects, never people. I hate to admit how many times my tears fogged the camera lens. Frankly, my emotions are still in turmoil."

Nikki nodded. "What are you doing in Florida?"

"I live here. Didn't you know?" Sybyll laughed. "Well, I do seem to recall we were all holding our collective breath rather than talking that day over the volcano."

"Dodging lava and ash fountains."

"You trying not to be airsick."

"Unsuccessfully despite your expert chopper flying."

Cassandra interrupted. "Nikki's associate is a photographer for the magazine syndicate, Sybyll. This is . . ." She looked from Roman to Nikki, blinking inquisitively. "I'm sorry, I don't seem to recall your name."

Nikki waited to see how Cantrell would do on his own. He didn't disappoint her; his response was smooth and clever.

His tone was treacle as he shook Sybyll's hand. "A pleasure." He noted her firm grip. "I'm too embarrassed to say my name or even admit to being a photographer in your presence, Miss Fields. I have your newest portfolio on my coffee table. It's well thumbed and enjoyed."

He deftly manipulated the conversation. "I see you're dabbling in video." Roman crouched to inspect the camera pack. "Nice outfit. I've seen the end products from this system; they're broadcast quality."

"Cassie and I are working on a project for her drama class and—"

"Yes," the professor interrupted, motioning them toward the massive sofa grouping that dominated the room. "I persuaded Sybyll to try a classics video. My students are doing some original short plays in pantomime. The mime was an ancient Greek form, and instead of elaborate costumes and words, the girls are using masks and gestures to get their ideas across." Cassandra sighed and rubbed her temples. "We were examining the first installment of what appears to be a monumental assignment."

"No, Cassie, the monumental assignment is getting those girls to stop wiggling and giggling and start acting."

She laughed. "You're right about that, Sybyll. Can I get you two some refreshments?"

"No thank you, we're fine," Nikki said. "You have a beautiful home with a stunning ocean view."

"And a rather eclectic mix of furnishings, some

of which are historically significant, if you're at all interested." When Cassandra saw Nikki's nod, she continued. "The Oriental pieces were brought over from China just before the Boxer Rebellion; the carpets are from the Middle East. There are a few Egyptian artifacts that a great-great-uncle smuggled out. I was told George Washington wrote a letter to Thomas Jefferson on that cherry desk, and there are a few antiques cornered here and there that predate the American Revolution."

"Art deco too," added Sybyll. She pointed to the Masks of Dionysus that adorned the area above a coquina fireplace. "Cassie's shy about her own contribution. Aren't they masterpieces? Note the depth of comic and tragic expressions carved into the reliefs. A priceless find."

"A lucky find," Cassandra said, then laughed. "I'd separated from my group in Greece and came upon this odd little shop southeast of the Acropolis, and there they were. We had rubberized copies made for my students to wear in doing their mime and are creating a duplicate of the Theater of Dionysus in the auditorium. It's quite . . ." she finished with a wave of her hand before settling heavily on a mauve sidechair. "But I'm sure Miss Holden is not here to interview me about the decor of my house."

Nikki relaxed into the plump cushion and crossed her legs. "Well, this would certainly make an interesting spread in an issue of *SouthEastern Homes*."

"But not today," the professor announced emphatically. "Today I think your interests are more sports-oriented. Correct?"

"Correct."

"I think this is my cue to depart," Sybyll quickly interjected. "Cassie, I'll edit this tape and call you later. I know this won't be a final product. We have . . . what? Two more rehearsals?"

"No. Just tomorrow night."

"Okay . . . I'll . . . oh, no thanks," Sybyll's deep voice halted Roman's gallant gesture of picking up the video equipment. "Got to get used to hauling around an extra twenty-five pounds. Quite a change from thirty-five millimeters. Come on, Cassie, you can walk me out."

Roman waited until the two women disappeared into the hallway. "Still convinced the professor is my client?" He stood before Nikki, rocking back and forth on his heels.

She contemplated his insouciant expression and matched it with one of her own. "The lady does teach drama and I know how good an actor *you* are." Watching him throw up his hands, she couldn't stop herself from smiling. "I must admit, you got out of giving your name rather nicely."

He grinned and said, "I did, didn't I?" Roman's dark eyebrows moved up and down. "Well, I think I'll just park myself over in the far corner, pretending to measure the light rays, and listening with enamored breath while you ply the secrets out of the fair Cassandra."

"Impressed you, did she?"

"Not as much as you do." He chucked her under the chin and strolled off.

"Are you sure I can't get you both something to drink at least?" Cassandra Topping inquired as she breezed into the living room. "No? Well, then, Miss Holden, I suppose we'd better get on with this interview."

The petite professor, curled up elegantly in the mauve chaise longue beneath the masks and other Grecian artifacts, prompted Nikki to think of nymphs. Those lovely maidens of mythology that were friendly and kind to mortals but could sometimes take revenge on those who hurt the people and things under their protection. She wondered if an errant husband would fall under that rule.

She became acutely aware of Cassandra's every movement and facial nuance. Both, however, proved to be quite serene. Nikki pressed a miniature tape recorder into operation and tried to project an image of equal composure. "First, let me tell you the slant of my article. Actually"—she stopped and smiled—"it's to be a series. One will be a profile on Ignace with sidebars on the game of jai alai, history, rules, betting procedures, and the fact that the pari-mutuel betting on the game reaches into the half-billion-dollar figure.

"Profiling Ignace makes me interested in you. How you met? I understand it was in Spain, a little about the romance, his adaptation to living in the States, and your reaction to becoming a... well, a jock's wife."

"A jock's wife... hmmm." Cassandra regarded the only man in the room for a moment, discovered that he was engrossed in one of Sybyll's earlier portfolios, and felt a bit more uninhibited. "You know, that's an interesting occupation. I read a book written by the wife of a baseball player and was shocked to discover the things she'd put up with. Never. That was my motto but, well, I guess I'm getting a little ahead of myself, right?"

Nikki contained her surprise at the woman's sudden display of nerves and remained quiet, watching her regain her poise to continue. "I guess the place for me to start is two years ago in Spain. I was on sabbatical. It was July and I'd gone to the Fiesta of San Fermin in Basque Country. Then Pamplona and the running of the bulls. I was caught under a Hemingway spell, or perhaps the spell of two incredibly beautiful dark Spanish eyes. Ignace was wildly romantic, and so were our surroundings.

"He seemed a very mature twenty-four and I felt I was a very youthful thirty-five. At first I was flattered, and more, I guess, even grateful by his attentions." Cassandra's laugh was sardonic. "I'm sure, Miss Holden, that you, too, have sung the national anthem of single women: 'Where have all the good men gone.' That colored my normally level-headed reactions.

"Normally level-headed... yes... that was me. A true schoolteacher. I was studious, bookish, and totally involved with my work, especially my dissertation. Yet here I was, being swept off my feet by this very dashing, very continental, very charming sportsman. At any rate, one tempestuous moment led to another and there the two of us were, less than six days later, standing in front of the village priest being married."

Cassandra shifted her legs, reaching for a half-filled glass of lemonade that was on the table. She sipped the warm beverage but found no refreshment and returned it to the moisture-drenched mosaic coaster. "Ignace is exactly like his name. It's a wonder the Basque school didn't throw him out. He was always brawling, arguing about the rules, and, as I'm sure you know, the rules are strict. The players are not allowed to show emotion in public, fines are heavily levied if a helmet is thrown. They are clean-shaven, forthright men.

"To the players, jai alai's honesty and integrity is something special. It's not just a job or a sport, it is a way of life. Ignace followed in the proud tradition of his grandfather and father, who were legends in the Basque school. His dream had always been to play in Miami."

Nikki cleared her throat, but it was the professor who voiced the question she intended to ask. "You want to know if he married me just to get to

Florida quicker than the usual year or two required under the Spanish impresarios?" Blue-shadowed eyelids lowered. "Don't think I haven't wondered that myself. In my heart I desperately need to believe that it was love. That's what I concentrate on.

"Yes, I know about the groupies. They're young and forward and uninhibited, and yes I know my husband uses them. Why? I don't know that. Maybe ...maybe you could ask Masters and Johnson for their opinion on the male sexual appetite as related to the ego."

She smiled at Nikki. "Ego. You certainly have to admit Ignace has an inflated one. He is an exceptional frontcourt pelotari. You've seen him play. He grabs the rebo shots from the back wall and hurls the ball with such force that he sprawls headlong on the court.

"He gives two hundred percent. He shows off. He flaunts convention. Breaks rules. The audience eats it up. Bets are doubled, tripled. Everyone comes out the winner. Ignace. Paradise Island. The other players. And the bettors.

"This is heady stuff, Miss Holden, especially for a twenty-seven-year-old. Ignace is making big money and I know you know about his new million-dollar contract or you wouldn't be doing the articles. The money, the recognition, the adoration. You add all that up and you get an ego that fairly bursts.

"Maybe I wasn't stroking it enough. I'm going to be quite frank with you, basically because Sybyll assured me that you're judicious and honest. I've offered to give Ignace a divorce. He's turned me down on religious grounds. I've told him how hurtful his affairs are but he ignores my pleadings. He seems to delight in telling me the intimate details of his every coupling. No, I don't plan on gathering lovers of my own. I—I guess I take after my mother."

Shaking hands tucked a stray wisp of blond hair beneath the turban. "My . . . my mother used to beg. She married a member of European royalty. Ignace and I are virtual duplicates of my parents' courtship and marriage. Perhaps all European men have the mistress habit?

"I keep hoping things will turn out better for us than they did for my parents. Ignace is glorying in his peccadilloes and they certainly don't seem to be affecting his performance on the court. Maybe when that happens, maybe when some of his endorsers begin to question his personal appetites, maybe—" Cassandra's smile was fragile. "*Maybe* seems to be the byword when you're a jock's wife."

Nikki Holden responded with a conciliatory nod, then angled for new directions. "What about you, Professor? Tell me about your interests, your work, hobbies?"

"After the woman behind the man?" Her expression was rueful. "I haven't changed since my marriage; my main focus is still my work." Cassandra's voice became dreamy, her complexion bloomed. "I was promoted to dean of dramatic arts at L'Ecole last year. The students are a joy. They are all girls, ages seventeen to nineteen. L'Ecole offers itself as a buffer, a thirteenth grade, for . . . well, again let me speak frankly, the crème de la crème of society's children who are treated to something extra. There's a three-year waiting list.

"I have an ambitious program for them. This month we are doing the Greek pantomimes. Very exciting and very gratifying. If you're interested in seeing how the woman behind the man works, please feel free to come to the school any evening this week and watch me work. Sybyll is having fun putting this video together. She keeps referring to it as my Dionysian *Thriller.* I know she'd love to spend more time talking with you."

"Thank you very much for the invitation," Nikki said. "It certainly sounds like an ambitious project for the both of you. I might just surprise you and show up. Between your lovely home and your personal interests, you'd make an excellent subject for an article." She watched Cassandra preen. "I'm curious about one other thing. Your name?"

"Mother went back to using her maiden name when father died and, after her death, I legally changed mine. I'm the last of the southern Toppings. Although I'm sure there are a few, as the British would so politely say, sideslips wandering about, courtesy of a philandering relation."

Cassandra watched Nikki turn off the recorder. "Well, this wasn't as painful as I'd imagined. I'd heard you could be a ferocious interviewer."

The redhead smiled and said, "Depends on the subject and the topic. I didn't have to do much in your case. You answered every question I'd intended to pose."

"To tell you the truth, I found it very therapeutic and highly beneficial."

"Like going to a psychiatrist?"

"Much cheaper."

They both laughed.

"If it's any consolation," Nikki continued, "I've interviewed quite a number of sport wives. Groupies and ego-boosting extracurricular affairs are, unfortunately, pretty standard in every sport."

"Maybe we should get together and form a self-help group. I understand a few Hollywood wives did."

"There's a thought," Nikki agreed, pushing herself off the sofa. "Once again, thank you for being so generous with your time. I just may show up at your school this week and see how Sybyll's video is going."

"Fine. We'd love to have you." Cassandra glanced inquiringly at Roman as the three of them walked toward the door.

"Oh, don't worry," Nikki interjected, "I'll be sure our photographer calls you well in advance to shoot those photos. Good-bye."

Chapter Nine

"Interesting woman," Roman noted while they walked down the driveway. He glanced at Nikki, waited for a comment, but was rewarded with silence. Her only action was to reach up and free her hair from the tight confines of the knot. "Still convinced the professor's my client?"

She leaned against the door of the Blazer. "I know she's not." Nikki folded her arms; her gaze was direct. "I made a mistake with you, and for some reason it took me longer than usual to discover the error of my ways."

"My charming personality and animal magnetism get in the way?"

Nikki found it difficult not to acknowledge his grin with a smile, but she managed. "Don't flatter yourself, Cantrell. No, this was due totally to my ignoring the obvious and a slight touch of paranoia."

"I find that hard to believe."

"Allow me to enlighten you." She cleared her throat as if preparing for a press conference. "By accident I became privy to some very, well, let's call it, top secret information in three different areas that all centered around one person. *Your client.*"

Her hand came up, forestalling any interruption. "Oh, don't worry, I'm not going to waste my breath asking. I'll *tell* you.

"When I arrived in Miami, I needed to gather information in these three areas. I didn't get anywhere. I'm sure you know how frustrating brick walls can be." She watched him nod. "I prefer the direct approach, but when continually thwarted I have no compunction about digging into my bag of journalistic tricks and entering via a backdoor. That's where I ran into you.

"I knew all my brick walls and damned if any one of them couldn't have hired you. Well, I'm sure you can see my problem, Cantrell. It was like playing button-button...only with a shamus. And the intriguing question of who was nervous enough to hire him?"

This time Nikki did release a smile, but it failed to reach her eyes. "Talking with Alex Lazarus didn't really help. Oh, he went on and on about your missing-persons record, then tossed in the monkey wrench that currently you were taking on a wide variety of cases.

"That still left me in the clouds. So what next? Process of elimination. You could have been hired by the good professor to track down her errant husband and build a divorce case. That was, as I quickly saw, an erroneous assumption.

"Then there's the jai alai crowd and the players' manager. They've put up major roadblocks trying to keep me from interviewing Ignace or anyone else at the fronton. I wondered if you weren't working undercover as extra security for Pleasure Island but—" Nikki stopped, then shrugged. "I've discounted that.

"My original instincts were correct. Your target is Ignace's under-age, bottled brunette lover: Marcy Nathan. And your client is—"

"My client," Roman interjected, "as you've correctly surmised, is Marcy's very concerned, very traumatized mother." Abruptly, he grasped Nikki's arm. "And I don't appreciate the fact that Marcy seems to have been, shall we say, relocated."

"Yes, let's say that."

"For what purpose?" He persisted. "A reward? Or, hell, don't tell me you're going to try to exploit a parent's suffering for a story? That's supermarket tabloid feed and it's beneath you, Nikki."

She realized he was more sarcastic than angry, the hand on her arm was decidedly more caressing than punishing. Nikki certainly knew the difference, she was an expert on punishment and pain. Taking all that into consideration, she decided to drop her bomb. "A bereaved parent is not the interview I'm after at all, Cantrell. I doubt that Marcy's *mother* is suffering."

"That's a callous statement."

"Credit me some brains. Mrs. Nathan? There is no Mrs. Nathan. You know the truth as well as I do. Marcy is none other than the daughter of Leonora Reichman, the owner of Pleasure Island!"

Nikki heard Roman gasp and choke on a garbled expletive. She offered a helping hand. "Stop babbling! Take a deep breath and speak from"—she slapped his chest hard—"the diaphragm."

He did just that. "You knew all the time?"

"All the time."

"And you weren't just trying to be friends with a lonely, scared runaway kid?"

"Lonely? Scared? Runaway? I know runaways, Cantrell, and this kid isn't. Why compared to Marcy, Lolita was a virgin!" Nikki stared at him for a long moment, then shook her head. "Well, I'll be damned! From the expression on your face, I bet you don't know the whole score."

"What in hell are you talking about?"

"Cantrell, don't tell me you fell for Leonora Reichman's distraught-mother act!" Her tongue clicked. "Oh, what the heck, I'll fill you in. Leonora wasn't worried about something terrible happening to her daughter. Mama was steamed because daughter ran off with her latest love trophy, Ignace." Nikki laughed at his astonishment. "Don't tell me this is the first time you've ever dealt with the green-eyed monster? You've got an angry, jealous woman for a client, Cantrell."

"It's her mother, for crissake."

"You still don't believe in Webster's definition that all mothers express maternal tenderness or affection, do you? Marcy spirited Ignace right out of Leonora's bed. Now Mama wants to get even."

"What about Ignace?" Roman's tone was sharp.

"He's safe. His million-dollar contract was signed, sealed, and delivered, with no morals clause. He just lies back and enjoys all the attention."

"What about you? What's Nikki Holden's angle?"

"Winning."

"Winning what?"

"An interview. One-on-one with Leonora Reichman. Something she's never granted. Something that's damn vital to me right now."

"And how are you going to manage that?"

"A trade. Leonora wants Marcy. I have Marcy and I want Leonora. So I trade one oversexed nymphet of a daughter for an interview that leads to the story of the decade."

He stared at Nikki Holden, saying nothing. He took in the tumble of fiery curls and eyes that glowed. Nikki Holden appeared wild and untamed. Unholy.

For a brief moment she felt the stinging strength of his fingers around her wrist and heard the chill of his words. "Who's the mercenary now, Holden? Who's—"

"Please," her tone matched his, "save the pithy

comments and hold the pontifications. Guilt is not one of my stronger emotions."

"Do you possess any emotions at all?"

"I try not to; emotions only complicate things." She used the car door to move him out of the way. "Don't *you* be a poor sport, Cantrell. Nobody's going to get hurt." Her fingers snapped. "Say, I'll be glad to put in a good word for you with Leonora and you can still collect your fee."

"And that's that?"

Nikki shrugged. "I assume you'll bow out gracefully."

Roman slammed the Blazer's door. The smile on his very masculine face framed in the open window began to make her edgy. That feeling intensified when she heard the ruthless tone of his voice. "I'm afraid you're going to get more than you bargained for this time, Nikki. I don't bow out, gracefully or otherwise."

"You're bluffing, Cantrell," she announced cheerfully, snapping the engine to life. "You haven't any more cards to play."

"You might be surprised at what's up my sleeve."

Her only response was to power up the tinted windows, put the car into reverse, and drive away.

As he watched the Blazer turn south out of the driveway toward Miami, Roman felt the need to do something physical. The need to work off an unusually high adrenaline level. The need to—a wry grin twisted his mouth, his needs centered solely around Nikki Holden.

She was certainly a woman of conviction. Brash. Opinionated. Sharp. Daring. Confident. Witty. There was no doubt in his mind that she suffered from tunnel vision. Nikki had a let-the-chips-fall-where-they-may, do-it-to-them-before-they-do-it-to-you attitude.

Nikki Holden was him five years ago.

He had mellowed. She had not. Instinct told Roman that Nikki Holden never would. He respected that. Hell, he was even coming to admire that. He kept needing to know more about her and he promised himself that eventually he would.

Right now he had a problem. His client had lied.

Roman thought about Leonora Reichman. He'd flown to Las Vegas to talk with her solely on the pleas of a mutual friend. He hadn't liked Mrs. Reichman. But liking a client wasn't a prerequisite for agreeing to find a runaway and, to be honest, this wasn't the first time a client had lied.

There were a number of facts missing in this case. Leonora Reichman was known as the female Howard Hughes. So why was this interview vital right now? Story of the decade, Nikki Holden claimed. The sketchy information Nikki relinquished had succeeded in whetting his appetite. With that thought in mind, Roman climbed into the Jaguar and headed for the only person capable of appeasing his hunger.

Nikki kept checking her rearview mirror for Roman Cantrell's Jaguar. When it didn't appear, she pulled off the ocean shore drive in Pompano Beach and found a service station. While the Blazer was being gassed up, Nikki went to the phone booth and called Marcy Nathan. The receiver was picked up on the first ring.

"It's Nikki. Everything all right?"

"I'm bored," Marcy whined. "Ignace's at practice and HBO's rerunning a movie I saw last week."

"Any strange calls?"

"No." The girl hesitated. "Is that private cop still hanging around?"

"Showed up at my place at seven this morning," Nikki related, "been following me around all day. He's definitely looking for you." She heard Marcy sniffling. "Did you talk to Ignace?"

"Yes. He'll give you that interview tonight. He's coming back here around twelve."

"I hope you reminded him to be careful."

"He's taking your famous polar route."

"Okay. I'll see you later. Why don't you try MTV or the video arcade game that's hooked up to the set? Just don't go out," Nikki warned.

Taking a deep breath, Nikki strove to relax. Things were beginning to fall back into place. She'd have Ignace's interview at midnight. Leonora Reichman was due in Miami on Wednesday. There was absolutely no doubt in Nikki Holden's mind that she'd interview the lady.

Lady? Shark. Barracuda. Hell, didn't Cantrell have any scruples when it came to clients? Cantrell. She paid the service station attendant, climbed back into the car, and examined A1A for a silver Jaguar. Nothing.

Nikki wasn't sure whether the knot in her stomach was due to relief or annoyance. A little voice said the latter. That same little voice was giving her a headache the way it kept repeating: "mercenary."

Mercenary. She'd been called a lot worse. So why did Cantrell saying it make her feel so . . . so dirty? Hell, he should talk! What gall! And so damn pious.

Then she remembered the touch of his fingers on her arm, the sound of his voice, and the expression in his eyes. A weary hand came up to rub her face. "If I'd just explained things a little more clearly. If he were in possession of all the facts. If—hell!"

Nikki looked in the mirror, made a face, then resolutely edged the Blazer back into the southbound lane. "Twenty-nine is too old to start developing a conscience, Holden. You've got to stop letting Roman Cantrell sidetrack you."

Chapter Ten

The dashboard clock registered six-thirty when Nikki guided the Blazer into the condo's underground parking garage, tucking the car safely in its designated slot for the night. She felt refreshed rather than tired, despite the fact she'd spent the last two hours walking off frustrations at Omni International.

Shopping malls weren't her usual diversion. The Omni was special. It had an amusement center. And a carousel. Shc'd indulged in two rides and pink cotton candy. Whirling lights. Calliope music. The rearing black stallion that was always her choice.

Fantasy. The stuff a little girl's dreams were made of. Nikki smiled. At twenty-nine she might be too old for a conscience but not for carousels, cotton candy, and merry-go-round horses. She was owed a fantasy.

When she switched off the engine, reality attacked in a weary wave. "Food. You need food and a hot shower." Nikki gave her growling stomach a consoling pat. "Then you'll be good as new and alert for Ignace's interview."

Sliding out of the car, her heels hit the pavement. The sound echoed loudly, ricocheting off the cement walls and into the shadows. Her gaze darted down rows of parked cars and concrete columns. Nothing appeared out of the ordinary. The usual silence. She squinted at the light banks. Were the fluorescents unusually dim? Or was it her imagination?

Nikki inhaled deeply. Everything appeared normal, calm, secure. This was a security apartment, she reminded herself. So why the sudden anxiety? She'd walked these same twenty-seven steps to the elevator for the last month. Knew them by heart. There was nothing different tonight. Nikki swallowed hard. Was there?

Pressing for the elevator, she listened to it make its usual slow descent and watched the lights countdown from the tenth floor. When the door hissed open, Nikki was forced to step to one side to let the occupant out.

Occupant? Her mind registered *bear.* Grizzly. The man was enormous. Six foot six. Three hundred pounds. Black curly hair hugged his massive head and sprouted from his open shirt collar. His torso resembled a tree trunk; his arms, two-by-fours.

It took her an extra minute to realize the bear wasn't alone. His companion's reed-thin form stepped clear of the gigantic shadow. He was as fair as the other man was dark. Myopic, red-rimmed, wild eyes dominated his pinched face. Perspiration collected on his upper lip like a mustache.

Nikki offered a weak smile in greeting before hastily walking around them into the elevator. Hearing the blond mutter something and watching both men turn, her hand darted quickly for the control panel and the security of a closed door.

Bear's bulky arm effectively halted the elevator's operation. His black eyes raked her form. "You're Nikki Holden."

She cleared her throat. "Not necessarily."

"Yeah," the blond popped his bubble gum, his voice nasal, "that's her. The boss's description matches. Say, is that hair color for real?"

Nikki nodded. "But I'll be glad to change it."

He snickered. "Mr. B said you were one snappy broad."

"Mr. B?"

"Mr. Borgianno," Bear intoned. "He wants you. Now."

"How is Rudy?"

"Impatient." He reached inside.

She gave a shriek when two beefy hands efficiently lifted her up and out of the elevator. "Really, sir, I can walk. Honest! There's no problem, I'm only too glad to let you play chauffeur. Hey! My purse!" Nikki watched her leather clutch smash to the floor. "Wait a sec . . . that's real leather . . . Just let me get my stuff. Hey!" The contents rolled across the macadam and into the path of a car that had turned into the garage.

Roman had one leg out of the Jaguar before the shift had locked the transmission in park. He heard Nikki yelling and watched as her shoes went flying when she aimed a flurry of ineffective kicks at the gorilla's shins.

He wasn't exactly sure what he was shouting as he belligerently charged the group, but his mind vaguely registered three startled expressions and Nikki's slack jaw.

Roman cut loose with a roundhouse swing that connected on the side of the skinny blond's head. The blond went reeling backward, slammed into a BMW, and then slid down into a head-lolling, seated position.

Nikki was suddenly tossed free of the bear's embrace, landing rather sloppily against the elevator doors. She babbled at Roman, discovered he wasn't paying the least bit of attention to her, and decided there was nothing she could do but watch the melée.

The man mountain was bigger close-up than Roman anticipated. But a slow mover. His fist drove a punishing blow into the big man's ribs.

The only response was a grin.

Roman delivered a quick, hard jab to the giant's jaw.

The grin grew wider.

Cantrell rearranged his body into a forward stance. He punched again. Hitting the bruiser's neck with the knuckles of his first two fingers, swiftly followed by a knife-hand blow and backed with a side kick.

Nikki was impressed. Cantrell was definitely black belt. His actions were a choreographer's dream. Then she winced. The bear had weathered the martial arts attack. Grin intact. And responded with a simple but very effective left hook.

Roman staggered, knees buckling. He felt as though he'd slammed into a brick wall. Shaking his head and wiping the blood from his mouth, he was set to issue a tae kwon do kick that had once broken a brick, when the giant picked up his companion and lumbered toward a blue Mercedes.

A dozen seconds later the only thing that confronted Roman were exhaust fumes. He stumbled over to where Nikki was reorganizing her purse. "Who were they?"

"A couple of friends."

"Yeah, I noticed how affectionate they were." He rotated his jaw.

"I think they were just trying to protect me."

Roman gave her a look.

"Well, you did charge in like... like..." She didn't bother to finish, watching as he left her to return to the Jaguar, shut off the ignition, and take a bag of groceries from the rear seat. "What's all this?"

"Dinner. Get your shoes." He punched open the elevator door.

Nikki waited until the fifth floor before speaking again. "I was rather impressed by your heroic battle cry."

"My battle cry?"

"*Unhand that woman.*" She smiled on hearing him groan. "My knight in shining armor." Her fingers brushed the dust off the lapels of his taupe raw silk jacket. "For God's sake, Cantrell, fix your tie."

When Roman found himself staring into a pair of twinkling blue eyes, he shoved the grocery bag at her and did as she requested.

"I hope you're prepared to play chef, Cantrell, my cooking talents run to peeling the aluminum foil off frozen gourmet entrées."

"Yes, I know, but I'm sure you're talented in other, more meaningful areas."

She ignored his leer. "Always in there pitching."

"Don't I at least rate a repeat of this morning's kiss?" he inquired as they walked down the hallway toward her apartment. "After all, I did save you from—"

"Save me?" Nikki pushed the large brown sack against his chest. "Cantrell, you screwed up my evening! I—Well, well, look who's holding up my apartment door. Glad you brought enough food for three."

"Say, are you afraid to be alone with me?"

She trotted two steps ahead of him. "Hello, Alex, you're just in time for dinner." Nikki's smile faded the minute she saw his expression. "Uh-oh. What's the problem, Alex? You look like a fed. Polished face. Polished manner."

Alex Lazarus looked over her shoulder at Roman. "What happened to your face?"

"Two goons downstairs."

Alex raised an eyebrow. "Rudy Borgianno's men."

Roman shoved Nikki against the door. "Is that who sent them?"

"Here, let me get the lock, that bag might give you a hernia." Fumbling in her purse for the keys, she tried to ignore his continual stream of threats. "Aw, Cantrell, lighten up, you didn't lose any teeth. I told you they were friends."

"Friends?" He kicked open the door. "You call a mob boss a friend?"

"Rudy's a sweetheart. That was just his way of inviting me to dinner."

"And that walking mountain is your idea of Emily Post?"

"Well, he was a bit crude." Her smile faded and she sighed. "You know where the kitchen is, Cantrell, why don't you put some ice on your jaw."

"I'd like to ice you, lady."

Nikki held him off with her hands. "Temper, temper. We have a witness. A fed."

"I'll turn my back," Alex said dourly. "Hell, I'll hold her."

"I can see you two guys need a drink. That burgundy in the grocery bag ought to be just the ticket." She walked backward across the living room. "Cantrell, you can pour while I slip into something with a bit more protection." She slammed the bedroom door shut.

Alex was shaking his head as he followed Roman into the kitchen. "Hell, this just gives her time to fabricate another story."

"Yeah, she's great at that, isn't she?" He handed his friend a wineglass.

Chapter Eleven

Nikki spent twenty minutes in the relative safety of her bedroom, figuring the wine would either make Roman and Alex more belligerent or decidedly more mellow. She was counting on the latter.

When she finally emerged, she breathed in wonderful Italian aromas coming from the kitchen. The dining room table had been precisely set, and two men were peering into various cooking pots that bubbled on the stove. Both had removed their jackets and ties and looked naturally at home.

Her own stress level fell and she relaxed. "All we're missing is a roaring fire and a snoozing dog," Nikki announced cheerfully.

"I'm allergic to dogs," Alex returned, "but I fully intend to provide you with heat."

She winced. His features were still carved in granite. Nikki diverted her attention to Cantrell. "That smells delicious. What is it?"

"Food."

Her head lowered. It was going to be a long night. She bounced back quickly. "Come on, guys, this attitude is going to give me indigestion. I can't eat if my stomach's upset."

Alex squared his shoulders. "Nikki, Rudy Borgianno is not someone to jerk around. Neither am I. I don't know what you've stumbled into, but I'm going to find out. Tonight. Now, we can do this nicely over dinner, or I can get a warrant and seize your notes."

"Every bit of information I have is right here," Nikki tapped her temple. "I don't respond to threats, Alex, or intimidation. And for me, a jail cell is like going home."

The expression on her face told Alex that he held the losing hand. "Christ, you must have given my father one helluva time." Reaching for the wine bottle, he refilled his glass and took a seat at the dining room table.

"Don't say a word, Cantrell."

"Not even 'dinner is served'?"

"That I can take." And Nikki did. Two helpings of spaghetti al quattro formaggi and three slices of garlic bread. She was adding antipasto to her plate, when Roman's voice broke the long silence.

"I don't think they'd keep you in stir too long. The prison food budget couldn't take it."

"Very funny."

"Wine?"

"Water's fine."

"Not a drinker?"

Nikki's shrug was noncommittal.

"Saving it for us? Hoping we get so loaded that whatever story you rigged up in your bedroom will make sense?"

"The only thing I rigged up was this outfit."

"And very nicely too," Roman agreed, surveying her sashed jump suit. "Redheads look wonderful in pink."

"Flattery will get you nowhere. Besides, you only want to know where I stashed Marcy."

"Stashed? I think kidnapped would be—"

"Kidnapped!" Alex's balled fist hit the table and perked up the china. "Hell, Nikki, does Mathew Cortlund know what you're up to?"

"Listen, I'm not on parole anymore. I don't ask Matt's permission to do anything!"

"He is your boss and that gives him the right to—"

"Not a damn thing!" She interrupted. "Matt knows the way I operate."

"Above the rules? Breaking the rules?"

"Oh, Alex, grow up. Who doesn't break a few rules? Don't try and tell me you two are angels."

"Ever get the feeling you're on a treadmill with her?" Alex asked Roman.

"She does try and wear you down. The secret is to jump off."

"And land where?" Nikki inquired sweetly.

"On my feet." Roman's posture was relaxed, but his eyes radiated strength. "Definitely on my feet. Walking to the telephone. Calling Leonora Reichman. Telling her that Marcy is just fine and you're running a scam. She won't set foot in Florida, charity tournament be damned. There goes your interview."

"You wouldn't. You're bluffing."

"Not this time, lady. I just reshuffled the deck and dealt myself the winning hand." He reached over and patted her arm. "Don't be a sore loser, Nikki. You were the one who gave me the edge. You told me how vital this interview is. The story of the decade, you said. I can take it away just by pressing eleven little phone buttons."

Roman let a swallow of wine wash the sour taste from his mouth. He hadn't liked doing that. Not to Nikki. He was dreading her reaction. If she pushed, he'd shove.

Watching as she drilled the knuckles of her right hand into the palm of her left, Roman decided to press his advantage. "This has nothing to do with one-upmanship, Nikki. Nothing to do with principles either. I'm concerned about you. You're the important one here. Don't you realize how dangerous things could get now that Rudy Borgianno's entered the picture? I'd hate to read your obituary in the *Herald*. And, no, I'm not being dramatic."

Nikki wondered if Roman's concern was aimed at her or himself. After all, that phone call would certainly tarnish his luster. Then again, an hour ago he had risked his life to save her.

Her teeth snagged her lower lip. Damn. The last time she felt like this was when she'd been arrested for stealing. Trapped. Nowhere to run. No way out but the one being offered.

But what exactly was Cantrell offering? Protection? He kept hinting that he'd like something more. More, however, wasn't what Nikki was prepared to deliver.

What the hell! She'd always been able to con her way out of any intimate situation. Right now all that concerned her was preserving her opportunity for an interview with Leonora Reichman. So she decided to give Cantrell what he wanted and do it with a smile. "If you don't mind..." Nikki extended her glass toward Roman. "Wine is the only proper beverage when one is forced to eat crow." Alex's exaggerated sigh made her chuckle and relieved the pervading tension. "This is rather involved."

"Then don't start in the middle," Alex warned.

"All right, give me a minute." Her hand came up. "I'm just organizing facts, guys, not changing them! Jeez, such trust!

"I guess the place to start is Cape Canaveral. I was there three months ago doing an article on the big business of private launches. Just as I was leaving, I heard some gossip about a DBS that was being launched this summer. A DBS," Nikki explained, "is a direct broadcast satellite. A special high-powered satellite that will send a video signal to anyone with a small rooftop antenna.

"Now, I realize that scuttlebut in and of itself is nothing to get excited about. But that was before I discovered what a very special satellite this was and who owned it."

"And?" Roman pressed.

"Well, on the manifest—"

Alex jumped. "How the hell did you see a NASA manifest?"

"Listen, do you want to hear this story or what?"

"Pass me the wine bottle, Roman," Alex said as he gestured for Nikki to continue.

"The manifest was marked SportPak Enterprises. For a while I thought this was nothing more than twenty-four-hour sports from around the globe. But on a hunch I had Matt Cortlund run it through a few channels. When all the perfectly legal, dummy corporations were cleared away, SportPak Enterprises turned out to be Reichman International. I had a gut feeling this satellite was not going to send golf matches over the airwaves.

"What were they planning to send? On the surface it did appear to be a simple communications DBS. There was even some talk about subleasing a few transponders to Western Union and a TV network. Perfectly legal."

Nikki's gaze shifted from Alex to Roman. "But those rumors turned out to be from a source at Reichman itself. I knew then that there remained a very big stone unturned. I did more digging. Found lots of rubble. Then... then a few gold nuggets began to glitter.

"First was the fact that the SportPak satellite was made by a subsidiary of Reichman International, VidComp; that the DBS had twenty-four super high-tech communications transponders that were capable of sending both video and audio signals and had interactive features.

"So, VidComp was my next target...and guess what? VidComp had just installed interactive gambling equipment, poker, blackjack, and dice machines at Leonora Reichman's Pleasure Palace in Las Vegas.

"The machines are handled by a central computer system. The casino loved it. No salaries or benefits to pay and minimum maintenance. The customers loved it. Instant winning, virtually cheat-proof, and no waiting. Plus it was familiar. Nearly everyone has played an arcade video game. This time, when you dropped in your money, you had the chance to win it back in spades!

"Well, VidComp was also busy setting up an interactive consumer channel on cable TV in Vegas. There was a onetime start-up fee of twenty-five dollars and a monthly charge of ten dollars for six hours of use. Consumers could transact a variety of business through the use of a rented dedicated terminal or their own personal computer that had been fitted with a modem and the appropriate software.

"Without ever leaving your recliner chair, you could transact various banking functions, order event tickets, catalog items, make airline and hotel reservations, and even send electronic mail. There are similar interactive systems all over the country. Qube in Ohio and I believe there's one here in south Florida."

Nikki took a deep breath, her gaze swinging from Roman to Alex and back to Roman again. "Say, I hope you guys are getting all this because there's going to be a test later."

Roman grinned and said, "Yeah, we're following but are you going somewhere with this or just running laps, Nikki?"

"Just hang in there, Cantrell, I'm going for a medal." She took a sip of wine, then continued. "Okay. Let's see . . . mmm . . . other gold nuggets began turning up. A sports reporter colleague noticed some big changes going on at the Pleasure Island complex here in Florida.

"Along with the regular quiniela, perfecta, trifecta, and daily double action, more exotic wagering was being introduced. There's Super 6, where a recent payoff was four hundred thousand dollars, and Monday Millionaire, where on the last Monday of the month some lucky person could win a million-dollar jackpot.

"This for both jai alai and the dog track, plus a Madison Avenue media blitz touting Pleasure Island as the perfect convention and resort center. How, you ask, does all this compute?"

Nikki smiled at them. "Again, Pleasure Island is Reichman International, and, it's been unprofitable since the day it was constructed. I went all the way back to 1967.

"Leonora Reichman was then Leonora Carter. A mover and shaker in south Florida, especially when it came to casino gambling.

"Legalized gambling was big business in Nevada and a new law was passed to allow corporations that sell stocks to the public to buy casinos and hold licenses. The push for a casino amendment was on once again in Florida and petitions were circulated. Was there any doubt that casinos would line the beach in two years?

"Not for Leonora. She was determined to be in the forefront, even though she'd have to do it silently. How? Well, she needed three things: money, land, and rezoning. Complicated? Not for this woman.

"Enter Councilman Raymond Peterson. Dapper. Charming. A gambler. A boozer. And a womanizer. What more could Leonora want?

"She played to his every vice. He got a half-million-dollar bribe to get her a license to construct a dual jai alai–dog track fronton plus a convention center that she ultimately planned on turning into a casino.

"Peterson, blinded by greed and lust, was talked into buying a tract of beachside land through a dummy corporation that Leonora would purchase back and he'd again reap a handsome profit. The councilman successfully had that site rezoned and just waited.

"All the while, Leonora was busy hedging her bets. She became involved with German industrialist Helmut Reichman. Reichman came in silently and purchased what essentially was nothing more than pilings in Biscayne Bay. Then with the same construction techniques that had just created the manmade Isle of Notre Dame for Montreal's Expo and a few well-placed gratuities, he began creating Pleasure Island.

"Ironically, Leonora fell in love with Helmut. When he offered marriage, she had to get rid of the councilman. She leaked that he was involved in bribes, rezoning, and land ownership. Councilman Raymond Peterson disappeared on a wave of scandal.

"The Reichmans didn't get off scot-free. The casino amendment didn't make it. Miami already had two jai alai frontons and other dog tracks and what was so exciting about another convention center? They tried to sell it. Three times. But all three sources proved to have had mob ties. So, no sale. And so the Reichmans had to hold on to it. In 1976, Atlantic City went for casinos and Leonora thought Miami would too. But in 1978 the casino bill was again rejected. There was nothing to do but keep Pleasure Island as a tax shelter, for the glamour and for the neverending promise of legalized casino gambling in Florida.

"Then Helmut dies in a plane crash and Leonora takes over. To give the devil her due, the lady knows her business. Reichman International begins to grow. Twelve companies dealing in resources from electronics to oil to aluminum to an emerald mine in Colombia. Everything she touches turns into gold. Everything but Pleasure Island.

"From what I've read about Leonora, it still galls her that Florida didn't enact casino gambling. She doesn't like to lose. Especially when it comes to money. So, she decided to outsmart the State."

Roman's eyes narrowed. "Outsmart the State? How?"

"By going over the heads of officials here. Way over their heads." Nikki smiled and paused for a dramatic effect. "Satellite betting."

"Satellite betting!" Alex echoed. "Nikki, you are nuts. There's not even a rumble—"

"Oh, the government will know eventually. The eighty-eight-million-dollar business expense on her federal tax form would be a dead giveaway."

"Are you sure?" Alex watched her nod vigorously. "Hell, I don't believe it. I can't believe it. Hell, shouldn't we draw the line at the heavens?"

She snickered. "Alex, if you recall, the last man who touted that line lost the presidency. Nothing is sacred."

"Jai alai's too fast a game," Roman inserted. "It's tough to cover. There have been a few special events on cable but the game loses its impact when you can't see the damn ball."

"Super slow motion, Cantrell. Even more advanced than they used during the last Olympic coverage."

He held up his hand. "Don't tell me, Reichman International—"

She nodded and finished. "—has a video products company that's developed a broadcast camera capable of making jai alai a spectator sport. Leonora's already taken the needed step to make the game a household word. She's given the American sports fan a champion they can both jeer and cheer."

"Ignace."

"Right again. Leonora's very clever. She started slow. Used Ignace's bad-boy reputation to pique interest. She's created another McEnroe. Sought out endorsements and sweetened the pot by signing him to a million-dollar contract."

Roman whistled.

"She'll start leaking information to the press shortly," Nikki related. "Oh, and if you're wondering how Marcy's running off to join Ignace will affect all this—it won't. Like I told you before, Ignace is no fool. His contract was in *his* best interest and at the time it was written, he was warming Leonora's sheets. You want to know something, Cantrell, I'm betting he crawls back into her bed very soon. Marcy's deluding herself. She's nothing more than a brief fling. That guy's fruit is always burning in his looms."

He choked on a laugh. "Well, you've got to hand it to Leonora. Even if a casino amendment does get passed, she's still covered." Roman shook his head. "This is big bucks."

"Very big," Nikki agreed. "And the return rate gets bigger when you stop to consider that it's her companies that built the satellite and the rocket. So Leonora's only cash outlay is private industry to use the launch facilities."

Her index finger stabbed the table. "Look what she's getting a piece of in Florida alone. Last year over two billion was spent on legalized gambling, ninety-eight million of that was wagered on dogs and jai alai. Just think of the untapped billions available when people are able to bet by pushing a button attached to their television sets."

"I am thinking," Alex mused. "Thinking of the billions that won't be going into organized crime's gambling coffers." He stared hard at Nikki. "Rudy Borgianno."

"He is the man in charge down here," she said. "Does he know? Well, I can tell you this much, Rudy has become very interested in jai alai. Or more correctly, one player. Ignace. Why? That I don't know. I had intended to find out tonight, but my hero"—she inclined her head toward Roman—"interrupted the plans."

"The thanks one gets for laying one's face on the line."

"Aw, Cantrell, don't fret. That yellow-green jaw doesn't clash too badly with your shirt."

"Was that all you and Rudy were going to talk about?" Alex persisted. "Before you answer, I happen to know that it was Rudy you were a bagman for when he was booking numbers in Saratoga. And despite that explicit interview he gave you last year, you're both still breathing."

Nikki took a healthy swallow of wine before answering. "Rudy was small-time then. I was even smaller, only eight. If it wasn't for him, I would have gone barefoot and coatless that winter and the next two."

Quickly, she blinked away the memories and felt annoyed with herself for sharing that much personal information. When she spoke again, her voice was devoid of emotion. "Rudy was promoted to Cleveland and now he's enjoying the wonderful climate, great beaches, and the enormous natural resources of Miami. We've remained friends. But I'm no fool. I know what he is and he knows I know. We respect each other.

"But to fully answer your question, Alex, there was one more item I intended to ask Rudy. The Pleasure Palace in Vegas has been plagued by threatening letters. You know the type: words cut out of newspapers and pasted together, all having to do with fire bombings. So far, false alarms."

"Anything being sent to Pleasure Island?" Roman inquired.

"Not so far. Pete Raines is head of security and we've become good friends. I think—no, I know he'd have said something." Nikki shrugged. "The threats in Vegas coincided with the installation of the video gambling. Could be disgruntled employees."

"Could be someone besides you knows about the satellite."

"So? They can't stop the launch, Cantrell. No one can. The Supreme Court says outer space is fair game. It's perfectly legal. Once again, Leonora Reichman has hedged all her bets." Nikki hesitated a moment. "Well, boys, what do you think?"

"I wish Roman had brought two bottles of wine."

"I didn't plan on having to split it *three* ways, pal."

"Sorry." Alex's smile was rueful. "Now that I know all this, Nikki, I will toss and turn all night. Tomorrow I will go out, confiscate a marina, and feel much better. Feel in control."

"What about you, Cantrell? Still going to call Leonora?"

He shook his head. "You kept your bargain. I'll keep mine. So your interview will really be a head-to-head confrontation about the satellite."

"Right."

"That could be dangerous. You'd be—"

"I'd be what, Cantrell? Come on, Leonora's smart. She knows that I haven't kept this to myself. Hell, Matt Cortlund's been trying to get an interview with her via normal channels for the last month. The lady does not condescend to respond. No. I'm perfectly safe."

"But is Leonora Reichman?"

"Say, don't you try and pull a fast one, Cantrell. Screw up my story and be damned. I can be a powerful enemy too."

He leaned over and ran his finger down her nose. "Of that I have no doubt, Miss Holden." Roman stood up. "Come on, Alex, I'll take you out and buy you that second bottle of wine."

"Make it a Scotch. Double."

Nikki was caught off guard by the suddenness and ease of their departure. Her silence broke as they opened the door. "Hey, guys, you two can't leave. Who's going to do the damn dishes?"

Two A.M. Nikki noted the time on the stove's digital clock when she returned from her interview with Ignace. Two hours. Two very long hours spent with a man who was so full of himself that she needed three aspirin.

Ignace believed he was God's gift to jai alai. Even more important, he was God's gift to womankind. He'd made veiled passes at her while Marcy was in the room and one hefty lunge when the girl had gone to the bathroom.

And what had Nikki gotten out of the interview besides a headache? Not much. She rewound the cassette tape, listened for a few minutes, found his accented voice anything but soothing, and viciously punched the stop button.

Ignace had given her a load of glittered manure but very little substance. He'd casually dropped the fact that his wife refused to divorce him, but Nikki knew that was only for Marcy's benefit. She had garnered one coup: an invitation to snap pictures at jai alai practice the next morning. All on Ignace, of course.

Her thoughts centered briefly on Marcy. She wondered if the girl knew how asinine she looked draped over and curved along Ignace's body. Marcy's own lack of self-respect and morality readily colored the situation. Nikki's perspective of the girl hadn't changed. She was having no attack of conscience in using Marcy as barter for an interview with Leonora Reichman. Daughter was a chip off her mother's amoral block.

Nikki chewed the aspirin, washing down the bitter residue with water, then opened the refrigerator. From the butter drawer she removed a blue aqua mask. It was one item Becky Cortlund had sent that was frequently used. Nikki found the mask an instant refresher and a cure for tension.

Remembering the posted notice that the sidewalk was set to be jack-hammered at seven, Nikki collected two wax earplugs. She was totally determined that nothing was going to deprive her of a full eight hours of much-needed sleep.

Chapter Twelve

Sweat burned Roman's eyes and blurred his vision. He took the lock pick out of Nikki's doorknob, wiped his face, then tried again.

His excuse? Fear.

He stopped again. Rechecked his watch. Eight-thirty. Where the hell was she?

Roman had been on the beach since seven, waiting to join Nikki for her morning jog. Only she never showed. He'd watched the surf for an hour and ended up more agitated than calmed.

The parking garage was his next stop. Her Blazer was in its stall. Engine cold.

Dumping a quarter in the pay phone, he anxiously waited to hear Nikki's melodic voice. Nothing. Not even the answering machine. Just long, seemingly forlorn rings.

Then he'd gone upstairs. Jabbed the bell. Heard the echoes. Pulled out his tools.

Roman thought about last night, recalling his quick departure. He should have stayed. He wondered a lot why he hadn't. But he knew why. He had backed Nikki into a corner. Sure, she had come across with the information, but he hadn't been blind to her tension and stress.

Instinct told him it was time to leave. You couldn't crowd Nikki Holden. She demanded room.

Space. She needed to breathe. To relax. To regroup.

He gave that to her, hopeful that his next approach wouldn't be feared. That it might even be welcomed.

So, why the hell wasn't she welcoming him now?

Could she have gone out after he'd left?

Rudy Borgianno. The name flashed neon-bright. He might have sent his gorilla back with another invitation. Or come himself.

And just maybe Rudy was no longer the sweet old mobster Nikki was counting on. He could have changed. For the worse.

Finally, the door swung open. The interior of the apartment appeared perfectly normal. Quiet. Shadowed. Sleepy. Nothing out of place. Nothing broken. Last night's dishes were on the counter. Clean. Pans were stacked in the drainer.

Nikki's desk was the same. Cluttered organization.

Absolutely normal.

So why wasn't he able to shake off this overwhelming feeling of dread?

Roman paused, palms flattened against the bedroom door, a rueful twist to his lips. "Hell, knowing Nikki Holden, she's probably breaking into *my* apartment and I'll find exactly what I did yesterday: an empty bed!"

But the bed was not empty.

There was enough sunlight seeping through the drapes for Roman to make out a body on the bed. A body that was not moving.

His mouth went dry, his muscles contracted. His hand crawled along the wall, fingers groping for a switch. He'd hoped the chandelier would illuminate a lie—tossed clothes on top of pillows.

It didn't. There was a body. Nikki Holden's.

She was sprawled, facedown across the bed. Her left arm dangled lifelessly off the mattress;

nightshirt twisted around her body; legs tangled amid striped sheets.

Nikki Holden had put up one helluva struggle.

Roman swallowed back the vomit that rose and burned in his throat. He knew the rules. Don't touch a thing. Call the police. But in this case rules didn't matter.

He forced his mind to unfreeze his legs. Carefully, he edged around the bed and discovered a pillow on the carpet. Her copper hair nearly obscured her face. The little skin he saw was blue. Cyanosis. Nikki had been smothered.

Dropping to his knees, Roman reached out to her. His hands visibly trembling as they hovered above her arm. Remembering how warm and vibrant she was last night, his fingers loathed to touch her cold flesh.

Her body was anything but dead.

Roman's brow puckered, eyes narrowing in discovery. Her skin was warm. Soft. A strong pulse beat contentedly in her wrist. Leaning closer, he heard a snuffled snore and discovered the blue tinge was an eye mask.

That's when his palm slapped her ass.

Nikki's eyelids slammed open. But she saw only black. Her arms and legs became a whirling mass. Her left hand slashed through the air, connecting with a disabling chop to whoever had hit her, while her right hand jerked off the aqua mask.

"Cantrell!" She saw Roman's mouth move, heard nothing. That's when she remembered the earplugs. "What the hell did you say?"

"Ouch!"

Nikki watched as he rubbed the same side of his jaw that had been bruised last night. Her eyes and voice held no sympathy. "Just what are you doing in here while I'm sleeping?"

"Is that the way you sleep? Hell, I thought you were dead."

"Dead? Dead!" Exasperated, she yanked at the sheets, kicking her legs free, then groaned audibly when he rolled onto the bed next to her. "Give me a break, would you, Cantrell?"

"Give you a break? Lady, I just lost twenty years!" He took a deep breath. "You weren't on the beach, didn't answer the phone. I didn't know what to think."

Roman's hand cupped her chin, turning her face toward him. "I came up here...and seeing you so lifeless, so dead..." He saw a softening in her expression and decided to take a chance.

His mouth claimed hers. When she didn't pull away, he decided to press his advantage. The instant his arms took possession of her body, Roman knew intense satisfaction. And relief.

His hands slowly mapped her womanly curves. His tongue teased apart her lips. Their breath mingled. Roman felt alive, invigorated, invincible.

Nikki's initial pleasure suddenly turned to fear. Not of him. Of herself. It was a foreign feeling. But one that she couldn't afford to ignore. She twisted her mouth free. "You...you're making a mistake, Cantrell."

His cheek rested on her breast. "Doesn't feel like it to me."

She lifted his head, her gaze direct, tone emphatic. "Well, you are." Nikki used considerable strength to pry him away.

Pushing back her hair and straightening her nightshirt, she tapped his watch. "You did prove rather useful this morning."

"As an amorous alarm clock?" He caught her smile as she left the bed.

"Exactly. I have people to see and places to go this morning."

Roman sat up. "Sounds like we're going to have a busy day."

"The hell *we* are!"

"Lady, I'm sticking to you like glue. Super glue."

"Even that has a solvent."

Nikki decided Roman Cantrell was certainly a man of his word. Despite the fact he was keeping a respectable distance, she found his shadowy presence personally debilitating. "Ignore, ignore, ignore" was proving to be her new mantra.

She waved a greeting to Pete Raines, watching while the fronton's security man unlocked the glass side door. Nikki couldn't help noticing how shaky Pete's fingers were this morning. He seemed unusually frail, his uniform swamping his lanky form.

"How are you this morning, Miss Holden?"

"Fine, Pete." She held up her camera case. "I get the privilege of snapping pictures of Ignace during practice." Nikki gave him a wry grin. "Noticed you were having trouble with your hands this morning. Anything serious?"

"Old arthur-itis," he joked. "Been with me so long, I've personalized it. Some days the medicine just takes a bit longer to work. Doesn't help that the air conditioner turns my office into a Frigidaire."

"You should speak to the management."

"They've got other problems. Bigger ones. Listen, miss, last night"— His voice shifted to a whisper, then stuttered—"It . . . it . . . it's that detective again." He glanced over Nikki's shoulder.

"Cantrell." Nikki patted his arm. "Be a sport and give him a hard time, Pete." She winked then headed for the jai alai court.

* * *

Settled comfortably in a rear fronton seat, Roman focused on Nikki Holden. She certainly knew how to handle a camera. Her angles were varied. The shots would be creative.

She also knew how to handle Ignace. Almost better than he handled the speeding pelota. The whirling dervish of sportsdom was a fast worker when it came to the ladies.

Verbally, however, Nikki copped the advantage. Two hours later her control terminated when an irate Ignace threw his helmet at her. The wire mesh screen played savior.

"Ever think of interviewing Dale Carnegie?" Roman inquired.

"Do I need a course in winning friends?"

"Maybe one in dodging flying objects."

"That I know how to do quite well." With the camera case firmly on the chair cushion, Nikki began to carefully repack the lenses.

"I'd have thought Marcy would have calmed him down."

She snickered. "Castration wouldn't calm Ignace. He's got the libido of a guppie."

He laughed and asked, "Another exposé in the works?"

"Not an exposé, Cantrell, reality. You're not in possession of all the facts."

Roman sat up straighter. "I thought you came clean last night."

"You didn't ask about Ignace," she reminded him sweetly. "And no threats about running to Leonora. Our deal has been consummated."

"Consummated? Don't I wish."

Nikki's groan was interrupted by Pete Raines, who handed Roman a cordless telephone. "Your office."

"I let them know where I was on my car phone,"

he explained, pulling out the antenna and pressing the appropriate button.

"We get to watch James Bond at work, Pete." Her eyes rolled expressively before she zipped the camera case shut. "How's the hands?"

Pete flexed them. "Like a kid's. Say, if you're finished here, how about coffee? I've got some information that might interest you."

Idly, she wondered if it was going to be another of Pete Raines's "I remember when" sessions. Her response, however, was intercepted by Roman.

"Nikki, Leonora Reichman's coming into Miami on the three o'clock plane."

"Two days early? Hell! I'm not ready. I, oh, damn." She stopped running her hand through her hair to stare at him. "You did it again, Cantrell, screwed up my timetable. Did you think you were helping or is this still the old one-upmanship at work?"

"Wait a minute!" He reached for her arm but missed. "Nikki! Hear me out." But she was running out of the theater.

For some insane reason Nikki had thought she could trust Roman Cantrell. True, he hadn't exactly reneged. He hadn't told Leonora not to come. But her arriving two days early was just as bad.

The Reichman interview needed special handling. Leonora was going to need to be confronted with documented proof before she'd admit the truth.

Nikki had only three hours to get prepared. Her evidence was in Matt Cortlund's safe in Chicago.

She navigated the Blazer through Miami's crowded noon traffic, deciding to use a pay phone in case Cantrell had gifted hers with a bug. She found immediate comfort in hearing Mathew Cortlund's familiar growl. "Help."

"Name it."

"Is the corporate jet sitting around collecting dust?" Nikki asked.

"Not if you need it. What's up?"

"Leonora Reichman's arriving here in three hours."

Matt whistled. "How'd that happen? We were set for Wednesday."

"Roman Cantrell."

"You sound"—he hesitated a second—"more disappointed than angry, Nik."

"I am. You know, I was beginning to like the guy. Even trusted him. But why he thinks he can run *my* show—"

"Positive it was him?"

"Who else? Not Marcy. Or Ignace. And Cantrell knew the score." She sighed. "I'm a lousy judge of character, Mathew."

"The hell you are!" He drummed his fingers against the receiver. "All right. Say, I could Fax it to the *Herald*. You'd get it in two hours."

"But how many prying eyes might see the photocopy? I think for this item we'll be much safer with a bonded courier."

"Fine. Where can it be delivered?"

"I'm headed back to the condo. I've got some research notes to plow through to help me organize my questions. Don't you worry, Matt, I won't let Cantrell or anyone trip me up." Nikki's voice hardened. "The Leonora Reichman interview is all mine."

Nikki found her apartment door ajar and heard a sprightly symphony of violins, harps, and cellos. She pushed inside. "If you think music will soothe this savage beast, Cantrell, you are sadly mis—"

"Don't edit William Congreve, Nikki." A deep

voice scolded. "The correct phrase is: Music has charms to soothe a savage breast."

"Rudy!"

"Ah, but you were expecting this... Cantrell?" Rudy Borgianno's silver brow lifted. "He was the one who annoyed Duncan?"

"Who?" She was walking toward him when the front door slammed. Whirling, Nikki saw the giant who had waylaid her in the parking garage. "Duncan, I presume."

"Yes, and Edgar is around here someplace, using your facilities. I understand the boys were a bit too enthusiastic in delivering my dinner invitation."

"Nothing an evening with Miss Manners couldn't cure." Then Nikki looked him up and down and smiled. "You look very dapper, very tan, and very tropical in that ice cream parlor suit. The climate agreeing with you?"

"In Miami, only the sun gives heat." Rudy embraced her, planting a kiss on each cheek. "I borrowed that from Mario Puzo's *Godfather*." He winked and stepped to one side. "Hungry? I brought lunch. No new business until after we've done justice to the caviar, the pâté, fresh fruit and cheese, and this excellent Pouilly-Fuissé."

Nikki had no alternative but to put her previous plans on hold. She settled companionably next to Rudy on the sofa, noting that Duncan and Edgar had taken sentinel positions in the foyer.

For nearly an hour they indulged in a game of remember when. Then, along with the food and wine, their memories dwindled.

"Seeing you now, Nik, I have trouble believing you were ever a scrawny street kid." Rudy tapped her nose. "You should have let me get that fixed for you."

"It was broken a few more times after you'd left.

Besides, even at the advanced age of twenty-nine I still have a nasty habit of sticking this nose in places where someone usually takes a shot."

"I subscribe to all of Cortlund's magazines just so I don't miss your articles." Rudy stroked his silver goatee. "You seem to lean toward sports news these days."

Nikki swallowed a mouthful of caviar. "That's why I need to talk to you."

"I'm more a fan of indoor than outdoor sports."

"Hmmm . . . rumor has it you've taken an interest in jai alai."

"An interesting game. Speed, skill, daring, and suspense. Plus lots of surprises." Rudy looked up from pouring wine. "I even tried to buy a fronton. But my pedigree wasn't quite up to inspection."

Nikki studied him for a moment. "That wouldn't have been Pleasure Island, would it?"

He nodded. "Of course, you do realize we are not having this conversation."

"Of course." She acknowledged the warning that registered in his dark eyes. "So now you're interested in Pleasure Island's newest asset."

"Ignace. Quite a high roller for someone so young. He likes flashy clothes, flashy cars, flashy women. A big spender."

"He's got a rich wife."

Rudy shrugged. "As I understand it, they are man and wife in name only. The professor keeps her bank account well out of his reach."

"So, you've been extending him credit. How far's it gone?"

"Half a million. The boy has a nasty habit of betting only on horses who are racing toward the glue factory."

"Five hundred thousand. That's awful deep."

His brow lifted. "I should be his conscience?"

"At that rate he'll spend more than he makes." Her blue eyes narrowed. "Ignace will be firmly in your pocket." When Rudy Borgianno smiled, Nikki was able to count all his teeth.

"My dear, you'd be surprised at how many people are firmly in my pocket. Rich. Poor. Bankers. Doctors. Lawyers. Politicians. Housewives. Scientists. Technicians. Lab—"

Nikki held up a hand. "I'm suitably impressed. What plans do you have for Ignace?"

Rudy's gesture was expansive. "*Che sarà, sarà.*"

"Still trying to acquire Pleasure Island?"

He massaged his goatee. "Interestingly enough, it's been yanked off the market. Leonora Reichman's been a very busy lady recently. We've been watching the improvements she's made at the Pleasure Palace in Nevada and the big money jackpots being promoted here."

"How do you feel about it?"

Rudy chuckled. "Am I supposed to feel?"

"Leonora's legalized improvements do steal from your registers."

"Do they?"

"Don't they?"

"Gamblers are an interesting breed. To them, it's a quick way to make money without the effort and discipline involved in working. They like the thrill and the tension, the daring, the challenge. They gamble for dreams." Rudy reached for some Brie. "It's a victimless crime."

"Is it?" Anger laced her words. "They're like alcoholics, Rudy. Sick. Mentally ill. And it infects their families."

"I never force anyone."

"Do you ever offer them help?" Nikki shook her head when she saw his expression. "Sorry, Rudy, I broke a cardinal rule. No moralizing." Her fingers splayed over his. "Forgiven?"

"Always. I do know where you're coming from. Remember?" He toasted her with the wineglass. "I'd be interested in knowing if you're going to use that same gambling line with Leonora Reichman when she hits town today." Rudy laughed. "You shouldn't be so surprised at my knowing."

"You're right, I shouldn't. But no, I have a more interesting hook for Leonora."

"What's that?"

With her chin settled on the sofa's back cushion, Nikki focused on Rudy's face. There was no tension in his eyes or his expression. The man was totally relaxed. "You already know."

"Do I?"

"She can't be stopped."

"Has the satellite been launched? No. Even if it does go up, you know how touchy electronic gadgets can be."

His finger flowed along her cheekbone. "Leonora Reichman can be certain of only one thing in life, and that's death. But that can be said for us all. And, Nikki, I'm sure the American public will be quite vocal once they read the facts in your article. Any chance of getting an advance copy?"

"Might be. Where shall I send it? Or will Duncan pick it up?"

Rudy smiled. He reached into his watch pocket and handed Nikki a card.

No name, just a phone number and street address. "I'll use it wisely."

"Never doubted that." He tapped his Rolex. "My, my, time flies when one is having fun. The Reichman jet just hit the runway. I won't keep you any longer, Nikki, we both have things to—" Rudy was interrupted by a scuffle in the foyer. "Duncan? Edgar?"

"Guys, remember this place is only rented," Nikki said as she pushed off the sofa. Instantly she was falling backward onto the cushions laughing because Duncan half-carried, half-dragged Roman Cantrell into the room.

"Redecorating in early neanderthal?" Roman asked breathlessly, his eyes never leaving the .38 special Edgar was aiming at him.

"Shall I dispose of the trash, Mr. B?"

"Christ, it speaks!" Roman grunted when Duncan elbowed him in the kidneys.

"Let me get my camera first, Duncan." Smiling, Nikki walked over and untangled the camera strap from Roman's arm. "Okay, now you can dispose of him."

"Hey! Wait a minute—"

"Why?"

"Because I've come bearing gifts."

"I own the camera, Cantrell."

"But I own an invitation to cocktails with Leonora Reichman, Miss Holden."

"Playing a game of give and take?"

"I never called her, Nikki. Honest."

She sighed. "Put him down, Duncan, no sense putting any more wrinkles in his suit. Say, is that a tuxedo, Cantrell?"

Roman looked up from straightening his lapels and grinned. "I'm hard to resist in this outfit. Besides, I thought you'd prefer the invitation in black and white."

Nikki rolled her eyes and nudged Rudy. "I'm beginning to regret not letting Duncan toss him out." She introduced the two men, then walked Rudy to the door. "Thank you for the gourmet lunch."

Again, he gifted her face with twin kisses. "My pleasure. Take care." Rudy nodded toward Roman. "If you ever need to borrow Duncan and Edgar, just call."

Leaning against the decorative divider planter, Nikki watched as Roman helped himself to what was left of her luncheon repast. "I noticed how respectful you were to Rudy."

"Mother didn't raise a fool." He scraped a cracker around the caviar bowl. "Borgianno's tentacles reach far beyond Dade County. Who knows, one of these days we might be in a position to do each other a favor." Roman chose the wineglass with a copper lipstick print and picked it up. "What did old Rudy have to say?"

"Nothing I didn't know. Ignace has expensive tastes and poor judgment. He owes half a million in gambling debts and the fair professor has cut off his monetary privileges.

"Rudy tried to buy Pleasure Island. He also knows about Leonora's satellite. So much for security, right? This story has got to get off the launching pad, and fast or—"

The door buzzer sounded. Nikki checked the door's peephole and discovered a uniformed courier. She patted down the pockets of her blouse, found a ten-dollar bill in her cream-colored trousers, and exchanged it for the leather attaché. "Finally!"

"What's that?"

"Evidence Leonora Reichman cannot dispute." She clutched the case to her breast. "Say, just how did you manage this little soirée with her, Cantrell? The lady's been on a jet."

"Ground to air phone. I said: Leonora we have to talk. She said: Fine. I have another more important job for you. Cocktails. Six. Black tie."

"Short and sweet."

"I didn't think *you'd* want me spending a lot of money talking to a woman you didn't admire."

"And what do you think Leonora's going to say when I show up?"

He grinned. "Actually, I've been wondering what you're going to say? How about—What's up, Mrs. Reichman?"

Nikki's smile peaked then faded. "I wonder what that new, more important job she has in mind for you is all about."

"We'll find out in three hours. I figure that'll give you plenty of time to put your evidence together, shower, and slide into that black silk strapless number that's hanging in your closet."

"And, pray tell, what are you going to be doing?"

Roman pointed to the food. "Eat this while I finish this." He held up a Stephen King paperback. "I've got the same one home, only three chapters to go." He tossed his jacket onto a side chair. "Nikki, don't just stand there, get to work."

It was ten minutes to six when Nikki finished dressing. She checked the results in the mirror and frowned. The dress was slinky and revealing. The bodice was high enough in the back to conceal her scars but the sweetheart front provided a mere iota of decency.

She took a deep breath. Gasped. Decided not to breathe again and left the bedroom mumbling. "This is not my idea of an interview dress."

Roman sat up and whistled. "It sure is mine. I like your hair that way. Long. Loose. Suits you. So does the dress."

"That's your opinion." She turned her back to hide a purely feminine smile. "Now comes the problem of fitting everything I need into this equally minuscule purse."

"Can I help? My coat pockets are available."

Nikki was handing him her small tape recorder, when the phone rang. "Yes? Hi, Matt, you just caught me. I—what?" She listened, nodding dumbly, then hung up.

Wide, disbelieving eyes dominated her face.

Roman grabbed her shoulders and gave her a sharp shake. "Nikki! What the hell is it? What happened?"

Chapter Thirteen

"Leonora Reichman's been murdered."

"Who says?"

"Matt." Nikki inhaled deeply. "He got it off the wire. Information is still sketchy. She was shot to death at point-blank range. Happened in the pool area at Pleasure Island."

"When?"

"Four forty-five."

"Let's get over there."

She grabbed her credentials, hesitated, then picked up Rudy Borgianno's card.

"Goddamn circus," Roman muttered. "Careful. Don't trip over that mike wire. Watch the guy with the Minicam. He's backing up."

"I see them." The wolfish greeting from a print reporter made her uncomfortably aware of her outfit. "This dress is a bit garish for a murder scene," she groused.

"Basic black, perfectly appropriate," he offered, then grinned as Nikki defiantly clipped her press pass to her décolletage.

She nudged his arm. "That cop waving at you?"

"Come on, I'll introduce you to one of Miami's finest." He led her into the cordoned crime scene as effortlessly as he'd gotten them into the outer barricade. "Nikki Holden, Lieutenant Mark Greene."

"Another charity bash, Roman?" the plainclothes detective inquired after shaking Nikki's hand and noting their evening apparel.

"Cocktails with Leonora Reichman."

"She's a tad indisposed. The medical examiner just wheeled her out."

"What happened?"

Greene shucked through his notebook. "Apparently, Mrs. Reichman was catching a few rays. Someone got close enough to shoot her. Once. Through the heart. Very neat. Clean. Left her seated nice-as-you-please in that deck chair over there."

"Professional hit?" Nikki inquired.

"Could be." The lieutenant's eyes narrowed. "Do you know something we don't, Miss Holden?"

She shrugged, expression blank.

"Anybody see anything?"

"Do they ever, Roman?" Greene's smile was sarcastic. "Her body was the silencer. There were three kids in the pool. Yelling and screaming over a water game called"—he looked at his pad—"Marco Polo?

"The poolside bartender was in and out, setting up for happy hour. Same with the waiters and busboys who worked the outdoor café. Everybody was busy. Nobody saw or heard a damn thing. We've got men going from floor to floor just in the unlikely event someone was looking out his window. But it happened between four-fifteen and five o'clock; most everyone was resting or getting ready for the evening."

"Find the gun?"

"Nope."

"Any prints on the chair or side table?"

"Hundreds. Drove the lab boys nuts." Greene leveled his gaze at Cantrell. "What about you? Was this business or social?"

"Business." Roman held up his hand. "Hold it,

pal, the only thing Leonora Reichman said was she had a problem. Nothing more. I don't have a clue."

Greene accepted that. Hesitated a moment, then in a low voice said, "Well, maybe I can give you a clue. Seems Pleasure Island's jai alai fronton was threatened late last night."

"That a fact?" Roman rubbed his mustache. "How?"

"Security guard got a letter. Rather religious in tone. The phone calls started coming this morning. We tapped the line. Guess what?"

"No more calls."

"Bingo. Apparently Mrs. Reichman believed it was serious."

"She's having the same problem with her Las Vegas casino," Nikki supplied. "So far, just letters and a smoke bomb in a bathroom, I think."

Greene scribbled a memo. "Anything else you can feed me?"

"Reichman Industries is a multi-million-dollar conglomerate, Lieutenant," she told him calmly. "Leonora gobbled up a lot of small companies to make hers big. She's not at the top of everybody's gift list."

"You think this murder was business-related?"

"Could be. Of course you might check to see what her five ex-husbands were doing," Nikki said dryly.

"Trouble there?"

She gave a noncommittal shrug.

"Shit. I hate it when some bigshot gets blown away," Greene groused. "All I find are tap dancers and vague innuendos. End up with a closet full of skeletons." He eyed Roman. "Care to dress a few?"

Nikki spied Pete Raines. The security guard was sitting at a far table, his hands wrapped around a paper cup. She drifted away from Roman and Mark

Greene, letting the busy milieu conceal her movements. "Want some company?"

He blinked her into focus. "Sure. Quite a to-do."

Whiskey scented and slurred his words. Liquor and arthritis medication had tinted his complexion slightly green. "Police question you?" she inquired pleasantly.

"Them. The press. Got my picture taken." Pete's hand shook as he raised the glass to his lips. "Hated it."

"With that handsome face?" Nikki teased.

His laugh was hollow. "Twenty years ago, yes, this was a handsome, much photographed face." He rubbed his jowls. "Today . . . hell, today I could be mistaken for a two-legged bloodhound."

"Men don't age, they get distinguished."

"Are you Irish?"

"Heinz 57. Why?"

"You've a gift for the blarney, Miss Holden."

Her hand settled companionably on his arm. "Tell me about the letter."

"I tried this morning."

"Sorry."

Pete took another drink. "Even though the fronton's closed on Sundays, I still have to make my rounds. Found it taped to the door when I locked up at midnight."

"What'd it say?"

"*Thou shall steal no longer. Repent or you will feel my wrath.*" He recited evenly, then emptied the glass. "The words were cut from magazines and newspapers. I'd been told to report anything like that directly to Mrs. Reichman. They've been getting letters in Vegas, you know." Pete sniffed. "*She* takes them seriously."

"The police didn't?"

"Only after I kept calling them about the phone

threats. Same message, Miss Holden, distorted voice. Male. First one came around noon."

"Just after I left today."

Pete nodded. "The phone started ringing as I was letting your detective friend out. Calls came every half hour till two-thirty."

"But none after the cops set up the tap." Nikki's brow puckered in thoughtful ribbons.

"Maybe the guy went to work," Pete offered.

"Maybe he had to get ready to hit Leonora Reichman." Her fingers drummed on the glass table. "Did you see her, Pete?"

"Briefly. She breezed into my office, asked what was what, gave me one of her regal nods, then disappeared."

"To relax in the sun."

He stared at her. "Sure. Why not?"

"Well, it's not as if the sun never shines in Las Vegas," Nikki said. "After all, her precious fronton was being threatened. Doesn't it strike you as a little odd that she'd sit in the sun?"

"Maybe she was meeting somebody. Maybe the person who wrote the letter and made the calls. Maybe they were going to make a deal."

"With no protection? I don't—"

"Perhaps her protection arrived a little late," Roman interjected.

There was no missing the self-contempt in his voice. "Come on, Cantrell, would you really have used that hunky body of yours as bullet proofing for a woman *I* didn't like?"

His knuckles landed a velvet punch against her jaw. "Thanks." He leaned closer to whisper into her ear. "*Hunky body*, huh?"

"Don't let it excite your main erogenous zone." She jerked her thumb at the chair Pete Raines had abruptly vacated. "Sit and we'll compare notes."

Nikki informed him of what the security guard had said. "Anything new?"

Roman shook his head. "The cops got nothing from interrogating any of the guests. The desk clerk said Leonora marched past him and went directly to the Presidential Suite. No entourage."

"That's the way she operates, Cantrell."

"Eccentric?"

"Self-contained. But a woman who always hedged her bets."

"Meaning?"

"Don't you find Leonora's actions rather relaxed? I mean, she comes winging to Miami, all upset about threats to the fronton, breezily checks out the security staff, then sits in the sun?"

He pursed his lips. "Leonora must have discovered that her fears were unfounded and the threats merely a ruse."

"And Leonora knew the person. Felt confident enough to handle him or her alone," Nikki added. "Of course, on that score, Mrs. Reichman made a mistake. Where's our hot-to-trot jai alai whiz?"

"At that hour I assume he was locked in with the other players."

"That is one heck of an alibi. Oh, damn, I forgot about Marcy. She's probably plugged into MTV. I doubt they interrupt for news bulletins."

"Sit down, Nikki, I told the lieutenant he'd find Mrs. Reichman's daughter in apartment eight-twenty at the Crestfall. Hell, don't look like that."

She sighed. "When did you find her?"

"Yesterday morning. Still doubt my skills?"

"No. Never really did."

"Don't go mellow on me now."

"Mellow? Wash your mouth, Cantrell. I'm just smart enough to recognize another perfectionist." Nikki ignored his laugh.

His hand cupped her chin."Why the brooding expression?"

"There's somebody I have to see."

"Another suspect?"

Eyes closed, she recalled something that had been said to her earlier: Nothing in life is certain but death. "I really hope not." Nikki stood up. "I'll be back. I want to talk to Marcy after the police; you should inform the lieutenant about Ignace and—stop shaking your head!"

"You are not going to Rudy Borgianno's alone."

"If I'm right, and you come along, who's left to make funeral arrangements?"

Roman scraped his chair back. "If you are right, I can think of nothing nicer than to share your block of cement for all eternity."

"What a romantic!"

"Is this Key Biscayne or Fort Knox? Did you count all those guards?"

"Ah, but how easily the magic of your name caused those Uzis and MAC-10s to be lowered, the electrified gate to be opened, and the hounds of the Baskervilles to be leashed."

"Cantrell, you'd better hope the magic doesn't vanish or we'll be ventilated, barbecued, and chewed when we try to leave. I don't suppose you're packing any firepower?"

"There's a forty-four Magnum in a hidden compartment under the dash."

"Six shots. Duncan won't even blink."

Roman switched off the engine. "Wasn't it you who said Rudy was just a sweet old guy? What changed your mind?"

"All the fully automatic people-killers." Nikki frowned. "I didn't fully comprehend his elevated status. The last time I saw Rudy was in Cleveland,

and it was nothing like this!" Watching the double front doors on the antebellum mansion open, she squared her shoulders. "Let's go, Cantrell, I don't think we should keep our host waiting."

Roman nudged her as they followed the houseman. "Seems Rudy doesn't hire anyone under seven feet tall."

"They need to be that tall just to dust the high ceilings. Jeez, this place makes the Vizcaya look like a barn." Her eyes moved quickly from the Olympic-size indoor pool that shimmered amid a botanical garden and colored lights to discovering one art treasure after another.

If it wasn't for Roman's guiding hand, Nikki would have broken her nose again, colliding with the butler when he stopped to open the ornately carved teak library doors.

"Twice in one day." Rudy embraced her. "I'm flattered. I see you're dressed for champagne."

"I thought Manhattans were your usual pre-dinner libation."

"A small celebration."

She noticed the TV, *sans* sound, was winking amid leatherbound books. "In honor of Leonora Reichman's death. Tell me, Rudy, was the celebration impromptu or planned?" Nikki heard Roman's swiftly drawn breath, but he didn't interfere.

"Anyone else had asked that..." Rudy Borgianno snapped the stem on a crystal glass and held up both pieces. "I am very disappointed."

She settled on the edge of his desk. "You'd have been more disappointed if I hadn't asked." Nikki glimpsed his smile and relaxed. "Was it you?"

"No."

"Anyone in your organization?"

"No."

"How about the threatening letters here and in Vegas?"

Again, he shook his head.

"The satellite will still be launched."

Rudy shrugged, pushed his hands into the pockets of his maroon velvet smoking jacket, and moved toward her. "Right now it's more important to know that *you* believe me."

Nikki's gaze skipped across the contents of his desktop. She picked up a lead crystal container filled with paper clips. "Mind if I take this? I'm all out."

"Not at all. How about that champagne?"

"A raincheck?"

"Anytime." Rudy escorted them to the front door. "What do you think of my home, Nikki?"

"Quite a palace. Next time I come, I'll want a Cook's tour."

Rudy's hand weighed heavily against her shoulder. "I know you, Nikki, you'll continue your investigation. But be careful. The killer is out there. Not in here."

Roman put the key in the ignition, turned it, then changed his mind and switched on the interior lights. Reaching over, he plucked the crystal from her hand. "Paper clips?"

"I needed them. Why, do you think the loss will dent organized crime's stationery budget?"

"Nikki . . ." Her stoic expression made him stop pushing. "You certainly are a cool one."

"Cool? Hell, Cantrell, I'm frozen solid. So, why don't you play hero, take me in your arms, and warm me up?"

"My pleasure."

He felt solid. Secure. Tangible. Luxuriating in the sinew of Roman's arms, Nikki felt her own strength being quickly restored. His callused hands were gentle against her bare shoulders. Her right cheek sensitively aware of his mustache as his lips caressed her jaw. "Thank you."

Roman leaned back slightly and smiled. "That's it? I thought cars were supposed to be romantic spots."

"Not front bucket seats with stick shifts that insist on mutilating."

"Oh, well, at least you know that I'm a push-over for an aggressive woman."

"Start the car, Cantrell."

"Where to?"

"Pleasure Island. Let's go see what the bereaved daughter and the oversexed jai alai player have to say."

Nikki waited under an enormous fountain chandelier in the lobby while Roman tracked down Marcy and Ignace.

"Everyone's in the Presidential Suite. Top floor."

"Everyone?"

"Marcy, Ignace, Lieutenant Greene, and a Reichman Industry lawyer." He was puzzled by her expression. "What's the matter, Nikki?"

"Ever notice how death and destruction brings out the masses, Cantrell? How silly of me! You of all people would."

"Want to translate that?"

"Sure. I mean, there you were, running food and medical supplies to Biafra years before it became the 'in' thing. The collective *we*, meaning the public, had to be treated to graphic visuals of starving children before we'd act. Same for Ethiopia.

"And missing children? Two million disappear every year, Cantrell, but when does it finally make an impression? Why, on the nightly news. As cameras bludgeon into homes with photos of thirty-two tiny body bags being unearthed from a basement, or the authorities fishing a child's severed head from a canal."

Nikki gestured around. "Look at tonight's crowd. Double? Triple? Dressed for a party. Oblivious to the patrol cars. Hell, maybe they're here because of those cars. Because of the news. Pleasure Island's a hot spot. Ah, murder, how it energizes the living." She looked at him and laughed. "Too cynical for you?"

Roman pushed her inside an empty elevator. "You must need food."

Eyes closed, Nikki leaned against the carpeted wall and tried to ignore the buzzing pressure building in her ears. "Maybe I'm just royally pissed at losing this interview. Losing the biggest story of my career."

"You're not that shallow."

Two silver-blue eyes opened. "The hell I'm not, Cantrell. I'm very single-minded. My career is me." A tawny brow arched. "You know what your biggest problem is?"

"You?"

"Correct. You've built a gossamer fantasy out of nothing but dirt."

Roman grabbed Nikki away from the elevator wall, his hands anchored around her upper arms. "Why are you trying to build a fight?"

"Am I?"

"Yes." His fingers threaded through the copper fire of her hair, lifting her face to his. "Yes, you are. And I know why. You're feeling guilty. Guilty about asking for a lousy hug in the car. Guilty about needing someone. Well, tough shit, lady, everybody needs someone. And you happen to be damn lucky to get me!" The elevator opened and Roman pushed

Nikki out. "Straight ahead. The gold leather door. For crissake tuck in your cleavage."

"I don't suppose you have any aspirin in your purse, Miss Holden?" Mark Greene's weary inquiry halted them in the foyer. When she shook her head, he gave a philosophical shrug. "How'd you get tangled with these mixed nuts, Roman?"

"A mutual friend."

"I'd dump him."

He grinned. "Who've you got in there that's doing all the yapping?"

"Little Marcy," Nikki answered for the lieutenant. "I'd know her whine anywhere."

"Whine? That's entirely too complimentary," Greene rebutted. "What a bitch! Demanded to see her mother's body just to make sure she was really dead. You'd never think they were related, much less mother and daughter. Never seen anything like it. You can smell the hate."

Roman watched Nikki's skin pepper with goose bumps. The room was anything but cold. When he attempted to move closer, she shrank away, wrapping her arms protectively around her midriff. His thumb and forefinger worried his mustache. "Who's she fighting with now?"

"Paul Taylor, Reichman's legal honcho. Marcy plans to replace her mother. Hell, the brat's all of seventeen and she tells him she's taking over Reichman Industries. Tonight."

Greene rubbed his stubbled jaw. "You might be interested in the fact that we had to cool our heels for half an hour; she wasn't at the condo."

"Where was she?"

"Out getting a pizza."

"Why the doubt?"

"Hell, Roman, she couldn't remember the place,

how long she was there, or even what she had on the damn pizza. The security man at the condo checked her out at four. With her attitude, daughter wouldn't have hesitated to knock off mother..."

The lieutenant made a face when a burst of Spanish erupted. "Another winner! Ignace."

"He should be off your suspect list, Mark. Wasn't he in the locker room?"

"Nope. Didn't arrive until five. Had a row with the team manager. Claims he was late because of a meeting downtown with some ad agency people over an endorsement." Greene shook his head. "Roman, according to the agency's receptionist, Ignace left at three-thirty and made her an indecent proposition on his way out.

"Christ, listen to them! I better get in there and play referee. Come on, I have a feeling I'll need help."

The Presidential Suite was the epitome of understated elegance. Roman quickly acknowledged that the occupants didn't equal their surroundings.

Marcy was cloaked in a perpetual cloud of smoke and her mother's gold leaf kimono. Parading back and forth as she issued regal dictums, she appeared more of a child than ever before.

Still wearing his jai alai uniform, Ignace sat behind an antique Queen Anne desk and was carving his initials into the polished cherry veneer.

The company lawyer was at the bar, shaking the last drops of Johnny Walker from a bottle.

"New mourners?" Marcy asked, clapping her hands together. "Oh, it's you two." She sashayed up to Roman. "So mommie dearest hired you to find me...." Her fingers pulled apart his evening bow tie. "Don't worry, Roman Cantrell, you'll get your check."

He slapped her hand away. "How comforting."

Marcy inflated her chest. "Show more respect. I own Reichman Industries. I have the power."

When the lawyer started to interrupt, she yelled him down. "Paul, you better go back and read my father's will. Reichman's mine. Held in trust. Everything's mine. Everything belongs to me." Marcy's calculating gaze settled on Ignace. "Well, darling, this makes all the difference for us." She ran her fingers through his ebony hair. "Your wife won't dare refuse to divorce you now. No, don't thank me." Her finger stilled his lips. "Paul, I want you to talk to Cassandra Topping tomorrow and—"

"I don't do divorces."

She walked to him, removed the glass from his hand, and threw it against the wall. "You'll do anything I tell you! Mop up that mess." Marcy fluffed out her hair. "This is nice. Very nice. I—"

"Aren't you afraid the person who murdered your mother will come after you?" Paul Taylor said, his words slurred.

Marcy turned to Lieutenant Greene. "Perhaps I should have police protection?"

"Have you received any threats? No. Then I'm sorry, Miss Reichman, but the Miami Police Department doesn't possess enough manpower to assign officers to everyone who *thinks* they might be murdered."

Trotting back to Roman, she blew a lungful of menthol smoke in his face. "Then I'll hire you. Mother thought you were capable. Nikki, I want you to do a story on me. How about: Teen Tycoon? Get Scavullo to do the photos and—well? Where is she?" Marcy stepped around Roman. "How rude! I think I'll buy out her contract and fire her. Hey! Where the hell do you think you're going, Mr. Private Eye?"

Roman didn't reply. He ran from the suite to the

elevator, but it was already halfway to the lobby with Nikki Holden. By the time he'd made his descent, she was nowhere to be found. Asking the overworked concierge if he'd seen a red-haired woman leave was a wasted effort.

Where had Nikki Holden gone? Why had she left? When would she turn up? Roman frowned, mentally sorting his options. The only logical place for him was her apartment.

Chapter Fourteen

Roman sat down. Stood up. Paced. Switched on lights. Turned them off. He made a sandwich. Took a bite. Couldn't swallow. Left it on the counter. Opted for coffee. But never poured a cup.

He checked the answering machine. No calls. Dialed to verify the time. His watch agreed. It was ten thirty-four.

His jacket came off. Shirt-sleeves rolled up. He attacked her Rolodex. Sorted through tiny white cards. Whom should he call? He snapped the lid closed. Returned to the kitchen and had the coffee.

Roman was sitting in the dark, staring at the luminous dial on his watch when the dead bolt clicked back. He lunged for the door and pulled it open. Nikki Holden fell into his arms.

She was drenched. Shivering. Her dress matched her hair. Both were soggy, limp, and smelled of salt water.

He said nothing. Picking her up, he kicked the door shut, then carried her into the bedroom.

Standing passively in the moonlight, Nikki was vaguely aware of the masculine hands that gently peeled off her clothes and cocooned her body in a quilted spread.

Roman lay beside her on the bed, holding her tight, waiting for the shaking to stop.

"I... I h-h-had t-to get out of th-there." Nikki caught her lower lip between her teeth, took a deep breath, and tried again. "I—I didn't like those people."

"The feeling was mutual." He stroked her hair. "All you had to do was ask. We'd have left together."

"You were being offered a job."

He snorted. "And *you* would have wanted my hunky body to protect Marcy?" Roman caught her weak smile. "So you went for an ocean swim?"

"Did I?"

His thumbs tenderly sculpted her cheeks. "You came home soaked and salty."

Nikki patted her body, discovering for the first time she was naked. "I'm dry now. And warm. Thank you." The hand she'd placed on his chest came away damp. "You're all wet too."

"Easily remedied."

She resented it when he turned away to remove his clothes. She needed to feel him close. The instant he pulled her back into his arms, she responded with a contented sigh.

"Nikki?"

"Hmmm..."

"Talk to me."

"About what?"

Roman tapped her nose. "What made you run tonight? And why to the ocean?"

Her eyes closed. "You won't understand."

"Try me."

There was urgency in his voice. And caring. And concern. It was real. Genuine. She searched his face, looking for something, for some sign. Then abruptly closed her eyes. When the truth was told, how could anyone understand?

"It was something Mark Greene said that was the catalyst," Roman mused. "I watched you change. Physically. Mentally. It was as if you crawled into a shell. Ah . . . I remember. He was talking about mothers and daughters and—"

"Hate." Nikki felt the inner pressure building again. She was glad Roman didn't try to stop her when she left the bed. "Greene was right. You could smell the hate in that room. Smell it. Feel it. Taste it. Choke on it.

"I tried washing it away." She shook her head. "Didn't work. Not even in the ocean. It will never go away. Mothers and daughters and hate." The chant went from vicious to desolate.

Her hands clenched around the quilt. "For Marcy . . . well, her hate is laced with jealousy, power, and greed. Marcy had everything. She wants more. She wants whatever anyone else has. Especially her mother."

"What about your hate, Nikki?"

"Mine?" She inhaled deeply. "My hate was twisted with fear and horror. I wanted nothing from my mother. But I got it anyway."

Roman sat up. "Got what?"

She dropped the quilt from her shoulders, allowing the moonlight to gleam across her spine. "Cigarette burns. Belt buckles. The big one? That's from a hot frying pan." Nikki heard his guttural response and felt his presence as he stood behind her. "Not sadistic reform school matrons, Roman. Just my mother.

"Actually, the matrons were quite nice. I had three meals a day. Clean clothes. A warm place to sleep. Sometimes I even got a toy. That's why I kept making sure I'd be sent back." Her laugh was hollow. "And Judge Lazarus was very accommodating."

He picked up the quilt and draped it around her. "Why . . . why didn't you tell someone? A . . . a teacher? Minister? The cops, for crissake!"

Nikki stared at him. "That was twenty years

ago, Roman. And we were a family who lived on the wrong side of the tracks. A family in constant turmoil. A family at war. Hell, even today the police are reluctant to get involved in domestic problems."

"This"—he touched her back—"Nikki, this wasn't simple domestic problems. This . . . Christ, this was sick, sadistic abuse. This was—"

"Two eighteen-year-olds—no, two children," she corrected. "Yes, two children who made a baby. A baby who shattered dreams of college. Dreams of fun. A baby who disgraced two families. A baby who disrupted lives."

Her voice went curiously remote. "The first three years were pretty good. My mother showed me off like a prize trophy. But babies have a way of turning into toddlers." She shrugged. "Maybe us redheads are more hyperactive than other kids. Maybe I was just too much for her to handle alone."

"What happened to your father?"

"He . . . he was a trucker. Local routes didn't pay as well as long distance. *He* wasn't around much. Then not at all. Disappeared."

"Other men?"

"Lots. *Uncles*, she'd call them. The shack we lived in was tiny. I . . . I heard things. Night after night. Day after day. Liquor made her loud. Lewd. Cruel. Tried staying out of the way. Sometimes it didn't work. The streets were safer. Survived there."

"What about school?"

"She convinced them that I was incorrigible. And I . . . I certainly did my best to prove her right. Shoplifting, purse snatching. I'd hide in the ladies' rooms and steal handbags from under the stalls. Trespassing, destruction of property . . . oh, hell, you read my rap sheet."

Roman shook his head, his tone bewildered. "I can't believe somebody didn't ask why."

"They just didn't. Nobody cared. Nobody wanted to get involved. Lazarus would pound his gavel and off I'd go. Relieved. Reform school was a vacation spot," Nikki whispered. "I cried when my time was up and I had to go back."

"How long did this last?"

"Too long. We were both getting older. She wasn't making the money hooking like she used to. Johns were few and far between. She kept drinking. And punching. This poor nose. Little cartilage. Lots of tape."

"When did Mathew Cortlund enter the picture?"

"He'd come to do a story at the detention center. His wallet looked fat. He caught me trying to return it after I'd taken the money. Instead of prosecuting, he made me work off my time in his office. He was publishing a hometown newspaper back then. Turned me into a general factotum. On weekends I'd work at his house or his track stables.

"I resented it at first. Two more people ordering me around. I had it all planned. I was going to rip them off, make enough money to really run away. A hefty grubstake. But I began to like Matt and Becky. And the work. And the praise. Lived for it. He paid me a token salary. So I stayed around.

"I'd pick the lock on the office door and sleep on the newspapers. Began reading them. Doodling questions. Editing stories. I was sixteen. For the first time I began to dream about a future. Dreams only lasted six months."

Desolation altered her tone and racked her body with chills. Quickly, Roman guided Nikki back to the bed. "Listen, you don't have to go on with this." He tucked the quilt around her, then pressed her head to his chest. His voice offered sympathy, understanding. "Memories can be damn debilitating. I know. I've had the nightmares. The shakes. Relived the horrors."

She squeezed his arm. "Yes... you do know what it's like."

Roman nodded. "Yeah. From safety to hell. You went from the cradle into the streets. I went from milking a cow in Nebraska to a foxhole spattered with my buddies' blood. Everything gets all mixed up. Right. Wrong. Life. Death. Fear. Anger. Hate. It all surrounds you. Permeates straight through to the soul."

"Soul?" Nikki shook her head. "I don't have one. Gave it up. No prayers were ever answered. I—I used to plan her death." She sat up, eyes gleaming. "I did. Late at night. Listening to her and her paying customers. Wondering if the liquor would make her sleepy or angry. I'd lie there killing her. Calmly. Coldly. Efficiently. And with an enormous sense of relief.

"You know what my big mistake was, Roman? Not murdering her. I thought staying away would please her. It didn't. Made her mad. Real mad. You see, she'd come up with this winning, money-making idea. Two-for-one."

"Two for one?" he echoed blankly. "I don't understand."

"Buy her. Get me free." Nikki saw his eyes close. "Great idea, huh? Problem was, I didn't think so. I boosted the guy's car. Took off. Cops nailed me. Thought they were doing me a favor by bringing me home instead of the station. I—I think it was some holiday.

"They said 'joyriding.' I insisted on grand theft auto. My mother and her friend said it was all a misunderstanding. They'd take care of me. They did—nearly beat me to death."

Roman was unable to contain his exclamation.

And yet he knew there were no words devised that could heal. He simply took her trembling hand, letting his strong fingers intertwine with hers.

She blinked reality into focus. "Woke up in the hospital... I don't know... days later. Matt had found me in the empty house. Couldn't remember what had happened. Better that I never did. They'd ruined me. Outside. Inside. Doctors had to do lots of internal repair work. But, what the hell, I'd have probably made a lousy mother anyway. Look what I'd had for an example."

"What happened to her?"

"Hopefully, one Kathleen Holden is dead."

"Never heard from her?"

"No. The Cortlunds petitioned the court to have me released into their custody. Been there ever since."

"What about your father? Any other relatives?"

She shrugged. "Vanished. None that I know of. Grandparents died before I was six. Nobody. Just Matt and Becky."

"And now me."

Nikki stared at Roman. "You? You're crazy."

"Why?"

"Because... because hell! I have nothing to give you or any man."

"How about yourself?"

Her free hand floundered in the air. "I'm a loner. I don't root. I live for my job. Beg for tough assignments. Enjoy wandering around the country. I breathe easier knowing that I have this freedom."

"I don't intend on taking any of that away."

She lowered her head. "I don't understand you."

"That's fine. I'll do the understanding for both of us." Roman's hand caught her chin, lifting her face to his. "This may sound corny and ridiculous, and quite frankly these feelings I have are totally new to me."

Nikki blinked. "Feelings?"

"Yeah. Like wanting you around night and day. Enjoying it when you cut me down. I've even begun looking forward to cooking your meals."

"You *are* crazy." Her tone was soft, wondering. "Roman, you shouldn't be wasting time with me. You need—no, you deserve someone . . . someone brand-new. With no past. No hangups. No scars."

"You're brand-new to me, Nikki. And who doesn't have scars? I know what I want." Pulling back, his gaze leveled into hers. "You."

He spread her fingers and placed them on his shoulders. "I'll be happy with as much or as little as you want to share."

Her right hand moved to his face; knuckles caressed a beard-roughened jawline. "For how long?"

Turning his head, his mouth kissed her palm. "Long as you want. Day by day. Hour by hour. You be the timekeeper."

"And when it's time for me to go?"

"Given half the chance, I intend to spoil you rotten. I'll make myself so indispensable, so needed, that you won't even consider leaving this hunky body."

His teeth flashed white; his grin was infectious. Her fingernail fluffed his mustache. "That a fact, Cantrell?"

"Indubitably."

"Show me." Her lips spoke against his.

He kissed her. His mouth slanting urgently over her half-parted lips, stealing her breath, savoring it as his own.

Then he relaxed, and began to take his time. Guiding her backward onto the bed, he luxuriated in the satiny feel of her lips and the honeyed nectar of her mouth. He enjoyed the touch of her hands pressing into his shoulders and back and the feminine fingers that tangled in the hair at his nape.

Her fears dissolved. Her inner trembling slowly gave way to a delicious sense of well-being brought on by the skilled mastery of Roman's caresses. Her fingers flowed along his spine and teased his sinewy buttocks with sensuous pleasure.

Roman's questing hands grew bolder as they cupped the generous curves of her breasts. His finger deftly woke a sleeping nipple; his lips and tongue proved erotic emissaries that awakened it to erect delight.

Nikki's low moans of pleasure intensified his ardor. His mouth rained kisses over her stomach, flushed breasts, finally settling possessively against her lips.

Her pliant body seemed to dissolve into the mattress as his hardened above her. Her movements came naturally. Thighs parting, hips arching, her hands guiding him into completing this most intimate connection.

Their sensual merger was so intense that they both gasped in unison. Roman savored the wonder and pleasure of their first loving bond. She felt complete. Full. Rich. Her body vibrated around his.

She felt him move inside her. Slow, delicate, careful strokes that showed he was fully absorbed in providing mutual pleasure. Nikki wrapped her arms tightly around his neck, clinging to his solid form, letting Roman take her to the height of fulfillment.

He lifted her hips, moving her even tighter against his boldly thrusting desire. He felt her fingers dig into his shoulders and heard his name cried in delight into his ears. His own body was totally out of control, surging and erupting in pleasurable violent relief.

As his weight came down on top of her, he kissed her mouth and tasted salty tears. "Nikki... what's the matter? You all right? I didn't hurt you, did I? I wouldn't. Never. You must be sure of that."

Shaking her head, she let gentle fingertips stroke away the concern that etched and distorted his features. Her own feelings of intimacy were so overwhelming that she found it difficult to speak. "No, I'm fine. Wonderful." She snuggled close into him. Her silken legs slithered intimately between his, her soft belly pressed against his flat stomach. "This was my first earthquake, that's all."

Sunlight and singing woke Roman. His watch said eight. Two hours later than he usually slept. He yawned, stretched, piled pillows under his head, and thought about last night.

He'd awakened at three and alone. Roman had found Nikki on the balcony, curled in a chair, listening to the ocean. With great difficulty he refrained from asking questions. Just held out his hand and experienced enormous relief when she took it and returned to share the bed.

She had been so quiet. So thoughtful. So totally introspective that her loud, decidedly off-key and missing-lyric rendition of "Let the Sunshine In" was truly music to his ears.

But it wasn't the tantalizing aroma of coffee or Nikki's cheerful "breakfast is ready" that caused him to bolt naked from the bed. It was her scream and the crash of glass that sent him running.

"What the hell is it? Nikki! Are you all right?"

Chapter Fifteen

Nikki Holden was standing in the middle of the kitchen amid chunks and slivers of glass and puddles of orange juice, clutching the morning newspaper to her nightshirt.

"Stay right there," he ordered. "Let me find my shoes and I'll come and get you so—"

"Don't you dare touch me!"

Once again icy eyes glared at him. "Nikki, what in hell?"

She snapped open the *Herald*. "Read this, Cantrell! Two more murders. Marcy. Ignace. And the jai alai fronton exploded. You should have helped. You should have stayed there. You should have been protecting her ass, not getting a piece of mine!"

With that statement Nikki threw the paper at him, boosted herself up on the counter, clear of the glass, and slithered out the pass-through into the dining room. "I can't believe this," she mumbled all the way into the bedroom closet. "For crissake, they're dropping like DDTed flies."

Roman followed her, reading as he walked. "It states here that the explosion and fire occurred less than two hours after the Monday night crowd departed. That would make it around two. The fire marshal says the fire appears to have been deliberate. Traces of an accelerant were found. A thirty-gallon storage drum of alcohol that was housed in the players' locker room was the source of the explosion."

He quickly scanned through some superfluous facts then slowly read the sidebar on the murders. "Seems the police found Marcy's and Ignace's bodies in his Porsche. Each shot once in the temple. The theory is that while they were in the parking lot, the arsonists must have discovered them and—"

Roman stopped reading when a fully dressed Nikki Holden ran by. "Hey, where the hell are you going? Nikki! Wait a min—"

She gave him a dismissing wave before disappearing into the hallway.

"Shit." Running a hand over his rumpled hair, he counted to ten, then went in search of his clothes.

Five minutes later the elevator doors opened in response to Roman's summons and revealed Nikki Holden sitting cross-legged on the floor. He bent down, cupped her chin in his palm, and lifted her face to his. "Well?" came his gentle inquiry.

Her eyelids lowered. "I didn't know where to go." Suddenly her mouth quirked. "But I suppose you'd like to tell me."

He grinned and said: "No comment." Then, helping her up, Roman guided her back inside the apartment. "Pour us some coffee while I exercise your telephone. Let's find out what the hell's going on."

Patience was also not to be found on Nikki's short list of virtues. And hearing only one side of a conversation, the bulk of it being "hu-huhs" and "I'll be damned" was aggravating as hell to her whirling mind. She attacked the instant he moved the receiver from his ear. "And?"

"Lieutenant Greene is a bit fuzzy from lack of sleep."

"Welcome him to the club!"

Roman tapped her nose. "Unfortunately, his reason was not as pleasant as ours." He'd be damned if she wasn't blushing.

"Will you please get to the point."

"The *Herald*'s account was quite accurate, Nik." Leaning back in the desk chair, he sipped from his third cup of coffee. "Definitely arson. Very controlled. The entire Paradise Island facility was evacuated, but damage was confined wholly to the jai alai fronton. Save a little smoke inhalation, no other injuries reported."

"Just two dead bodies." Her voice was derisive.

"Yeah." He slammed the empty cup on the desk. "Greene figures that Ignace was driving Marcy to his apartment. The sports car was parked in a remote area of the rear lot. They were sitting, talking, windows down, two people came up on either side, aimed and . . ." Roman's mouth twisted. "Never knew what hit 'em."

"What did?"

"Not the same gun that killed Leonora," he stated. "This was small, twenty-five caliber."

"Close range, though."

"If they were doing more than talking . . . say necking—"

"—or arguing—"

"—whatever, conceivably they were occupied enough not to notice they were about to become—"

"Victims," Nikki finished for him.

He eyed her closely. "Something bothering you?"

"Lots."

"You thinking about Borgianno?"

"Thought and then dismissed." She fingered the crystal paper clip holder on her desk. "Rudy's the quiet type. He was never one to take over in a blaze, no pun intended."

"He could have changed. Or maybe been told to

change." Roman rubbed his jaw, the rough growth of stubble scratching his palm. "I need a shave, shower, and fresh clothes." Roman pushed out of the chair and moved to her side. "Come with me." His arm looped her waist. "My house is right on Lauderdale's Intercoastal Waterway. Great place to think."

"I'd better stay here and put a call in to Matt." She made a face. "He's going to love hearing that everyone connected with this article is dead." Nikki cleared her throat and, feeling oddly shy, said, "Roman, if you'd like to bring some of your clothes and shaving gear here . . ."

Roman's smile grew broader. "Thanks. How about if I stop by the police station on my way back and see if Lieutenant Greene has anything new. I'll get copies of his reports and . . . well, maybe you could still salvage some sort of story."

"Sounds good." Her energy and enthusiasm were slowly building. "I'll give Rudy a call." Her hand came up. "Just a phone call and get his reaction. You can never tell, Cantrell, the man has a proverbial who's who in his pocket."

He wagged a finger at her. "I'll hold you to that phone call business. Frankly, Nikki, my trust runs shallow where Borgianno's concerned." Roman gave her a quick kiss, then headed for the door. Pausing, he turned back. "I've learned something interesting about you."

"What's that?"

"How and when you use my first name. And the intimate flavor it has rolling off your tongue."

She threw a paper clip at him. "Hey, Cantrell, don't forget to bring some food. I seem to remember you promising to cook."

"I thought I cooked pretty good all night long!"

He ducked out the door when a handful of clips were aimed in his direction.

"I was wondering when I'd hear from you," Mathew Cortlund said.

"Frankly, Mathew, I don't really know what to say." Nikki scratched her head, scowled as her fingers came away greasy and salty. "The mortality rate on this feature article is one hundred percent."

He merely grunted. "What do you want to do?"

"Take a shower."

"Do some thinking while you're in there," he said evenly, "I'll leave this entire matter in your capable hands. Whichever way you want to go—"

"Off the wall," she muttered. "This whole thing is totally off the wall." Nikki pulled herself together. "All right, I'll get back to you."

"Make it tomorrow. I've got a meeting in Denver today. Becky will probably send you a souvenir."

Nikki sat, chin balanced on piled fists, staring into space, thinking for a good twenty minutes. The result: nothing.

She reached for her favorite pen. Black. Sleek. A rolling ball tip that glided effortlessly across any type of paper. She let the doodles just happen.

An hour later, fresh from a shower, shampoo, and wearing clean jeans and a short-sleeve sweater, Nikki reexamined her creative graffiti.

"Bingo." She circled one and decided to check it out. "I just might be able to salvage something out of this mess."

Picking up the pen, Nikki started writing a note to Roman, then stopped. After all, she was merely going on a fishing expedition. What was there to say? She'd wait until she could actually serve up the prize catch.

* * *

It was quarter to five when Roman tried the knob on Nikki's apartment door. Busy juggling an overflowing grocery bag, a garment carrier, and a bouquet of spring flowers, he exhaled a relieved sigh when the door opened.

Spoil her. That's what he'd promised. Since he wasn't quite sure how she'd take to it, Roman opted to start small with flowers, slowly graduating to bigger things. Then again, Nikki Holden wasn't the type to be impressed by material goods.

"Okay, no cracks about the flowers. Or the time." He dumped the bags on the kitchen counter and peeked out the pass-through. "I wangled reports out of Mark and—"

Roman blinked twice at the shadowy figure sitting behind the desk.

It definitely was not Nikki Holden.

He rushed into the living room. "Hey! Who in hell—" The desk light clicked on. "Alex! For crissake, Lazarus, what's with the cloak and dagger?"

"Roman . . ."

"Listen, if you're after another free meal, pal, three really is a crowd."

Shaking his head, Alex moved to his side. "Roman, there's something I've got to tell you. You better sit down."

Brown eyes became wary. Roman's hands grasped fistfuls of Alex's shirt. "I want to know one thing—is Nikki dead?"

"No."

"How bad?"

"Real bad."

His hands fell away. His lean features constricted. "Tell me."

"The Broward sheriff found her around two-thirty on U.S. twenty-seven."

"Blood Alley?" Roman stumbled backward, groping for the sofa. "What happened? Details. How'd they get to you?"

Alex sat next to him, hand on Roman's shoulder. "Boy Scout hikers discovered her car. She was stuffed in the back. Beaten. Bad. Dead, they thought at first. Sheriff didn't know who. No purse. No registration. Nothing. Even the Blazer's plates had been ripped off.

"They found my name and the Crab Shanty's on a piece of paper stuck on the dash. Must have been from brunch on Sunday. Gave me a call. I helicoptered over."

Roman's breath rattled in his chest. "Where is she now?"

"I had the EVAC chopper bring her into Jackson Memorial."

"Let's go." As Roman slammed the apartment door, the last thing that registered was the bouquet of flowers lying on the kitchen counter.

Hospitals always made Roman Cantrell sick. The antiseptic smell burned his nose. A continual bing-bing invaded his ears. His eyes watched nameless, faceless white uniforms regroup and scurry in a dozen different directions.

"ICU's right down the hall."

He gratefully allowed Alex to play guide dog. "Did . . . did you call Matt Cortlund?" It was the first time he'd spoken since they'd left the condo. His voice sounded disembodied.

"Tried. All I got was his service. Didn't want to leave a message like this with them. I'll keep phoning and—whoa—" His arm came up in support of his friend.

Roman had to close his eyes. The last time he'd felt like this had been in Vietnam. He'd just killed a VC. His first time. He'd thrown up in a rice paddy.

Had nightmares. Daymares. All he saw was a screaming face. Never mind it was an enemy's face. It was the face of a man.

Nikki replaced that memory. But not with her bright, vivacious image. A new one formed. One that haunted. A picture that was sterile and white and horribly silent. A picture filled with tubes, bottles, clamps, and machines.

"Roman." Alex tapped his arm. "The doctor's coming out. Roman?"

"Yeah." He inhaled. "How is she?"

Dr. Hammond was busily scribbling notations on a chart. He clicked the metal binder closed. "Time will tell. Next six to eight hours are critical. We're monitoring her vitals."

"Did she say anything? Talk to you—"

"Talk! The lady's got a broken jaw. Concussion. Three cracked ribs. Punctured lung. We're watching the spleen. She took one helluva beating. Tire iron. Metal rod. I sent my report off to the sheriff and—" His beeper signaled. "I've got to call in. There's a waiting room by the elevator." He patted Roman's shoulder. "We'll let you know."

Dr. Hammond didn't put in another appearance until two A.M. "We're upgrading Miss Holden's condition to serious." He raised a hand. "She's still unconscious. Vital signs are steady. That's one tough young woman.'"

He scrutinized the two men over the top of his bifocals. "You two, on the other hand, look as though you were the ones beaten. Go home. Get some rest. Food. I can guarantee there'll be nothing new for today."

Roman rubbed a weary hand over his face. "Could I . . . please, can I just go in and—"

"One minute." Dr. Hammond extracted a pocket watch. "I'm timing."

Roman spent thirty seconds just staring. Nikki's jaw was black and blue. Stitches evident against the waxy skin of her forehead and chin. When the nurse moved to replace the IV bottle, he quickly blessed the tip of her nose with a kiss.

Alex was retrieving a quarter from the phone's coin return when Roman entered the waiting room. "Cortlunds must be at some party. Or on a business trip. Maybe I'll have better luck when his office opens. How she look?"

"Like hell but at least she's alive."

Alex watched him pace. "What's up, pal?"

"I know Nikki wouldn't want me to stand around here doing nothing."

"Just what is it you have in mind?"

Feet planted firmly apart, hands on hips, Roman eyed his friend. "How does the sheriff figure this?"

Alex scratched his cheek. "She picked up a hitchhiker and got rolled."

Roman snorted. "Does that sound like Nikki to you?"

"No." Alex's expression grew curious. "How do you figure it?"

"That she found the murderer and was taken by surprise. Are you sure there wasn't anything in the car. Any notes? Any—"

"Clean. But I'll be glad to double-check."

"Personally?"

Alex nodded. "Where'll I find you?"

"Nikki's."

Roman put the wilted flowers in a vase of water. He wandered aimlessly through Nikki's apartment. Tired but not sleepy. Hungry but not ready to eat. His body wanted action but his mind was scattered.

After a couple of hours of useless treadmill

activity, he ate, dozed, and was startled by the telephone. "Yeah?"

"It's Alex."

"I can hear it in your voice, pal. Nothing."

"Sorry. Nikki's Blazer was wiped clean. No prints. Just bloodstains."

"Too careful for a hitchhiker."

"I agree."

Roman checked his watch. It was six-thirty. "Do me a favor?"

"Anything."

"Keep trying to reach the Cortlunds from the hospital. I'll be calling you for updates on Nikki's condition."

"What are you up to, Roman?"

"Maybe I'll have some luck retracing her steps. See ya' later."

Retrace Nikki's steps. Certainly sounded brilliant when he'd said it a minute ago. Where to start?

Once again Roman assaulted her files. Everything appeared to be in perfect disorder. The Rolodex was opened to Matt Cortlund's private number. He tried it. Still no answer.

Roman spied the wastebasket. Settling it on his knees, he carefully examined the five crumpled scraps inside. Four were nothing more than Occupant generic mailers. The fifth was an office supply shop receipt for typing paper.

He smoothed the yellow carboned invoice. Nikki would need it for an income tax deduction. Roman took a deep breath and forced himself to keep thinking those positive thoughts.

Anxiety, anger, and fear steadily splintered his body and mind. He lashed out. His right arm scythed the desktop clean. Papers, files, folders, and the Rolodex went spiraling around the room.

That's when Roman noticed the blotter. And

Nikki's inked doodles. He stared at each initial: L.R.—Leonora Reichman. M.—Marcy and I.—for Ignace. "Suspects up the yin yang," he mused, "unfortunately they're all dead."

Roman viewed the etched heart that surrounded Rudy Borgianno's initials. "All right, Nikki, if you trust the guy, so do I."

The jagged line she'd drawn around the words: *Pleasure Island* ultimately decided his next step.

"I'll do exactly what you must have done, Nik. Return to the scene of the crimes."

Chapter Sixteen

Pleasures found.

Pleasures lost.

Roman surveyed the dismal scene. Tourists, conventioneers, and locals had departed Pleasure Island, taking their money. Fire officials still sifted through the rubble while police kept watchful eyes on the curious. Even the ocean breeze hadn't been able to dissipate the acrid smoke that smogged the area.

Searching the various official faces, Roman discovered a familiar one. "Morning, Mark."

A startled Greene nearly dropped his notebook. "Didn't expect you, Roman. Read the Broward sheriff's report. How's Miss Holden doing?"

"Still unconscious. Doc upgraded her from critical to serious."

"Well, that's good news." His smile faded as he stared at Roman. "What can I help you with?"

"Got anything new?"

The lieutenant went back through his notes. "Escorted the Reichman Industries lawyer to the airport about an hour ago. Paul Taylor was one happy man."

"Happy?" Roman nodded at the scene. "I know I'm a bit groggy, pal, but—"

Mark's smile was a sarcastic slant. "Those lawyers always get happy when the word *probate* enters a conversation. Taylor will pile up some big bucks getting the Reichman house in order. Seems, too, that both Leonora and Marcy were migraine givers. The board of directors were hardly ecstatic over what Leonora was planning. Something about launching a satellite?"

Roman shook his head. "Yeah, that was Nikki's story of the decade. She found out about it when she was up at the cape." He pursed his lips. "Say, did that lawyer happen to see Nikki yesterday?"

Greene shrugged. "Listen, I can yank him back but, hell, Roman, the sheriff's report said hitchhiker and—"

"Sorry, Mark, I don't buy that for a minute. She is not the type of woman to pick up a hitchhiker." His hand came up to massage some vitality into his face. Roman took a deep breath. "I'm positive that Nikki stopped here yesterday. Who'd you have on duty?"

"Clyne and Darnell. Why?"

"I'd like to find out if they saw her. Where can I find them?"

"Right here. Let's go ask." Greene led the way through the barricade and introduced Roman to the two uniformed officers.

"A tall redhead? Hmmm . . . yeah . . ." Clyne jingled a set of keys in his pocket. "Yeah. I remember her. Real friendly. Quite a biscuit." He cleared his throat. "No offense. She was asking about one of the security guards. I sent her over to talk to"—he turned and pointed at the coffee truck—"that young guy. Right over there."

Roman long-legged it to the wagon. "Say, uh—Curtis"—he read the name tag—"early yesterday morning, you spoke to a tall redhead. Ring any bells?"

"Sure . . ." Curtis mumbled around a mouthful of glazed donut. "Miss Holden, you mean."

"What'd she want?"

"Lookin' for Pete Raines. Poor old guy. All this hit him real hard. He put me in charge. Haven't seen him since, well... let me think..." Curtis frowned. "Why, I guess it was the night Mrs. Reichman was shot."

"Did you tell that to Nikki?"

"Yep. Gave her his address too."

Roman's eyes narrowed. "Okay, now you can give it to me."

Roman piloted the Jaguar to a small rundown multifamily wood house at the tip of Miami Beach. Colorful spray-painted Spanish graffiti was the building's only redeeming decoration.

Climbing the steps, he wondered if the rotted front porch would hold his weight. It did. With a crackling expletive. The buzzer was broken. So he opened the ripped, flapping screen door and walked in.

The house had the same smell as the hospital. Except for the disinfectant. Here, there had been no sanitary conditions in a long time. Dirt caked the windows. Dust carpeted the spare furnishings. Cobwebs draped elegantly from corners.

"Anybody home?" Roman tried not to gag as the stench of urine invaded his nose.

Harsh, spasmodic coughing exploded the silence.

Roman tracked the source to a small back bedroom and found Pete Raines vomiting in a coffee can. "Christ, you need a doctor." He looked around for a phone but couldn't find one. "I'll call from my car and get an ambulance over here—" An upraised hand quieted him.

"Got too many doctors now." Pete collapsed back onto a dirty pillow. He gurgled as he spoke. "Expected you sooner. Could have given you a harder time then."

"You're not making much sense. Give me a name, Pete. I'll call your doctor. How about medicine?"

"Too late for either." Coughing again seized control of his anorexic body. "Ahh . . . at . . . at least I was given enough time."

Roman crouched by the bed. "Time? Time for what?"

"Didn't she tell you?" Somewhere he found the strength to chuckle. "Still makin' you work, heh?"

"She?" He stared hard into Pete's face. "You mean Nikki? She was here yesterday?"

"That long? Nice. Nice of her to give me the extra time." His eyes closed, dry tongue tried washing cracked lips. "I—I suppose the cops are with you. Wantin' to hear it all."

"Yeah. Everybody's here. Waiting. Take your time."

"Not much left. Took me twenty years to get her."

"Her?"

"Leonora."

"Leonora Reichman?" Roman echoed in disbelief. "You? You killed her? But . . . but why, Pete?"

"Her laugh." Brown eyes opened briefly. "I kept hearing that laugh of hers. Night after night. Twenty years' worth. Beautiful woman but a lousy laugh. A cackle. Like a witch.

"Laughed at the end too. I showed her. I had the last laugh. I was in control. This time. I ruined her. She couldn't believe it was me, Councilman Ray Peterson. I won. I had the gun."

"I'll be damned."

"Got her. The fronton."

"You . . . you set up the explosion?"

He managed a weak nod. "Couldn't stand the place anymore. Should have been mine. Mine and hers. Now, now, it's nobody's."

Roman exhaled and rubbed his face. "You killed Leonora. Blew up the fronton. But the kids . . . Ignace and Marcy . . . why the hell did you—"

"Not me." Pete gurgled and spat into the coffee can. "No reason." He reached up and tried to grab Roman's shirt but couldn't find the energy. "She believed me."

Roman calmed him. "She? You mean Nikki?"

"Yeah . . . I told . . ." His voice and body were depleted.

"Told?" Roman snapped to attention. "What'd you tell Nikki? Pete!" He shook Raines's shoulder. "Christ, Pete, don't die on me yet! This is important. What did you tell Nikki Holden?"

"Dark. Crazy. No bodies. Just faces. Crazy white faces. Crying. Laughing. Just . . . faces . . . And then . . . wind. Beating wind." The coffee can fell from Pete Raines's waxen fingers. "Gone. Leonora. Fronton. All gone. Just . . . like . . . me."

Roman made two calls from his car. The first to Lieutenant Greene; the second to Alex Lazarus. "How's Nikki doing?"

"She's still in a coma but the doc said her pulse was a bit stronger. I'm going to try Cortlund's office when Chicago opens up in an hour. How about you? Any luck?"

"Yeah. Seems that missing councilman from twenty years ago . . . you remember, the one Nikki told us about. The one Leonora had bribed then threw to the wolves, was none other than the fronton's security guard, Pete Raines. The poor bastard has been planning her murder all these years. Finally was able to get close enough to pull the trigger."

"I'll be damned," Alex muttered.

Roman quickly told him the rest of Pete Raines's story. "You know, pal, I'm inclined to agree with

Nikki. I believe his story. He didn't kill Ignace and Marcy. I have a hunch who did, though."

"Need help?"

Stopped for a traffic light on Collins Avenue, Roman pressed a button under the dash. Reaching into the compartment, he extracted a .44 Magnum in a belt holster. "No, Alex, I've got all the help I'm going to need. See you soon."

The tropical rain forest vegetation proved to be an effective buffer, and made Roman thankful he'd been here before.

Number eleven. Beachside. Boca Raton. The iron gates swung open in quick response to a lock pick. He parked the Jaguar by the sundial. Then, after checking that his jacket concealed his gun, he punched the doorbell.

A soft-spoken, petite, Jamaican maid insisted: "Madame cannot be disturbed. Great tragedy here, mon. Her husband dead."

"I've come to pay my condolences." Roman physically moved her to one side, ignored her sputtered protest, and pushed open the doors to the living salon. "I never realized red was an accepted color for mourning."

Cassandra Topping struggled to free herself from the confines of an upholstered chaise longue. "Who the hell are you? Oh, yes, I remember you. The photographer. Mr. . . . Mr . . ."

"Cantrell. Roman Cantrell."

"Yes, well?" She tidied a strand of blonde hair that had slipped from her chignon and walked toward him. "I'm afraid you'll have to leave. This is hardly the time for a photo session."

He scrutinized the room. "Everything seems picture-perfect to me." His gaze shifted back to her. "Even the distraught widow. Pale complexion. Dark circles under the eyes. And those eyes so perfectly primed with tears. There goes one streaking down your cheek. What timing!"

"Really! I find you quite arrogant, Mr. Cantrell. Leave. Now or—"

"Ahh, I see death hasn't dulled your appetite, has it, Professor? The patio table is set for two hearty souls."

"That's because there are two of us eating breakfast."

Roman turned and discovered Sybyll Fields approaching from the foyer doors. "Hail, hail, the gang's all here. Were you here when Nikki Holden visited yesterday?"

"You're mistaken, Mr. Cantrell," Cassandra interceded. "Your Miss Holden was not here yesterday, nor have I heard from her since last Sunday."

But he paid little attention to the tiny blonde. His dark eyes never wavering from the ashen face of Sybyll Fields. "You should have taken Nikki's photo last week, Sybyll. So vibrant and full of life. Or perhaps a more emotional picture is etched in your mind's eye. Perhaps you'll always see Nikki as the bloody mass you stuffed into the back of a car." Roman saw a nerve jump by her left eye.

"Has something happened to Miss Holden?"

"Oh, that was very good, Professor." He turned and applauded. "Nice touch of surprise and concern. You must be an excellent drama teacher."

Roman wandered over to the fireplace. He stared at the bas reliefs of the Masks of Dionysus. Only one registered. He could swear he heard its mocking laugh ringing in his ears.

Roman smiled at the two women, who now stood side by side. "Life is not a Greek mime farce, Professor. And I'm no fool." The toe of his shoe kicked at a small Oriental carpet. "This is new. A bit out of place."

"I find a change in decor one of the great necessities of life."

Roman bent down and pulled it back. "Oh, Professor, what's this? Stains?"

"My previous maid was accident-prone. That's why I hired a new one."

"Looks like blood. Doesn't wash out, does it? Lady Macbeth had the same problem."

Lighting a cigarette, Cassandra settled herself on the sofa. "Blood? Hardly. Tomato juice. And yes, it is difficult to remove." She blew a lungful of smoke at him. "Is there a point to this . . . this interrogation, Mr. Cantrell?"

"Murder."

"Whose?"

"Your husband and his girlfriend."

Cassandra shook her head. "Sorry to disappoint you. That happened at . . . ummm . . . what time did the police say, Sybyll?"

"Two."

"Yes. Two." She smiled at him. "Well, we were rehearsing with our students until after one. Sybyll has it all on video tape. It would have been impossible for us to have driven from Boca to Pleasure Island in under forty minutes."

"Driven, no," Roman returned the smile, "but Miss Fields is a certified pilot with her own helicopter. I remember seeing a photo of it in one of her albums. Small and incredibly maneuverable. As I recall, there is a heliport pad on Pleasure Island."

"You are grasping at straws."

"Am I?" Roman stood in front of her, balanced on the balls of his feet like a fighter. "I figure it this way. You were the one who wanted a divorce. Ignace said no. Religion had nothing to do with it. He'd found the proverbial golden goose. Blackmail."

"Blackmail? I lead a very circumspect life, Mr. Cantrell."

He hoped the slight waver in her voice wasn't his imagination. "Circumspect, Professor? That's your biased view. Ignace knew that his wife, pillar of society, dean at an exclusive girls' school would pay and keep paying a lot of old money to keep her affair a secret."

"Affair?" Cassandra's laugh bordered on hysteria. "Check away, Mr. Cantrell, there is no other man in my life. There's just my work and my students."

"And they're very important to you, aren't they?"

"Very. They are my life. My sole purpose for living. And I'm a fierce protector."

Roman noted the expression on her face echoed the force of her words. He proceeded with cool calculation. "Then you'd hate to have the truth get out?"

"Truth? What truth?" She drilled her cigarette into a mosaic ashtray. "I told you, I am not having an affair with any man."

"I'm not saying *man*. I'm saying Sybyll. That's what Ignace was holding over your head. Just the vaguest whisper of your lesbian activities around your school and—"

Cassandra Topping vaulted to a standing position. "If you're threatening me, Cantrell, I'll—"

"You'll what? Kill me too?" He heard Sybyll Fields's sharp intake of breath and pivoted. "That's what Nikki figured out, came here, and confronted you both. By the way, she's not dead."

The lanky woman collapsed on the chaise. "She's...she's not?" Sybyll shuddered. "I...I'm glad. It happened so fast, that I—"

"Shut up, Sybyll!" Cassandra hissed.

She ignored that order. "I like Nikki. Really."

"Sybyll!"

"Oh, Cassie, what's the use?" Huge liquid brown eyes dominated her angular face as she returned her attention to Roman. "The other thing. Well, I'm not sorry. Ignace was a cruel man. Delighted in hurting Cassie. Drained her bank account. Took all the joy from her life."

She sniffed and groped in the pocket of her denim shirt for a handkerchief. "There was really nothing else to do with Ignace but kill him. We've been planning it for a while, when the Fates—well, they seemed to be on our side.

"We heard about the Reichman shooting and the bomb threat on the news. Then Cassie got a call from that girl...that Marcy. The snotty little bitch demanded a meeting."

Sybyll closed her eyes, her recitation was one of relief. "We...we agreed to a meeting out in the parking lot. A very late meeting. Ignace always parked his precious Porsche miles away from the building. It was really very simple. I helicoptered in. No one was around. Cassie did try to talk to Ignace but the fool had told that girl about us. And Marcy, well, she kept taunting and laughing about what the press would do with this information."

Her lashes lifted, her pupils were black pinpoints. "We were dressed in black leotards from the rehearsal, had Cassie's father's set of pearl-handled derringers, and brought the masks. It seemed appropriate. Now was going to be our turn to laugh and their turn to cry.

"Then the building exploded. Perfect! Fate! We thought the killings would look like just another assault on the fronton. But yesterday, when...when

Nikki came and—" Sybyll's breath caught. "Cassie! No! Please, not again, no more!"

Roman drew his gun as he whirled around. Cassandra Topping was less than a yard away, brandishing a poker in her upraised hand.

"Please... *don't* put it down." His two hands steadily closed around the grip. His aim was lethal.

Time ticked in slow motion.

He watched her hesitate a moment, elbows bending. Roman wondered what Cassandra Topping was thinking. Was she visualizing lurid headlines? Long trial? Murder sentence? The electric chair?

In his mind's eye he could see Nikki. Laughing. Teasing. Wild copper hair. Those potent, changeable eyes.

Another image formed. Roman tried but failed to push it away. Tubes. Machines. Nurses. His nostrils twitched in remembrance of the hospital smells.

He knew the law was soft. Knew smart lawyers were paid to keep clients out of jail. Knew guilty, wealthy clients could easily skip the country.

So when Cassandra Topping raised her arm and charged at him, Roman decided to satisfy them both.

He pulled the trigger. And was still dispensing tissues to Sybyll while the police read her her rights.

It was three o'clock before Roman was able to return to Miami's Jackson Memorial Hospital. He found Alex Lazarus beating time with a cute off-duty blond nurse. "How's Nikki? Any change?"

Alex nodded, pocketing a phone number. "From serious to stable. About half an hour ago. The doctor just went down to ICU. The Cortlunds are on their way. Rudy Borgianno just left. Interesting guy!" He peered at Roman. "Christ, you look like hell!"

"I had to put away Ignace and Marcy's killer." Roman's eyes were bleak. "Ignace's wife. She was the one who did this to Nikki." He caught sight of Dr. Hammond in the corridor. "I'll fill you in on the details in a minute."

He tagged the doctor. "I hear your patient is doing better."

"The nurse called to tell me Miss Holden just opened her eyes." He sucked in his cheeks. "I'll take a chance that the sight of you won't make her faint. You've got one minute."

Roman's hand trembled against Nikki's hair. He smiled into her eyes. "The doctor says you are going to be just fine. While you've been . . . resting . . . I knew *you'd* want your hero to be terminally sidelining the bad guys."

His smile changed to a grin as Nikki raised her eyebrows in mute understanding. "Wired jaw. I don't think I'm going to like you being so quiet. Oh, well, I've got a great blender at home. You'll be thrilled with the gourmet liquid meals I'll be preparing. We can just lie side by side in the sun and I'll watch you freckle." He kissed her nose.